The Hard Kill
A John Stone Action Thriller

by Allen Manning & Brian Manning
Cover by Allen Manning

Copyright © 2019 Allen Manning

CHAPTER

1

Great Falls, Montana

DAY 1   12:33 Mountain Time

"Welcome to the Jungle"
Guns N' Roses

Emily meant everything to him. She was his daughter, his whole world, and he would do anything to protect her. Frank Colt had struggled to adjust to a normal life since retiring from the Army. Emily's mother, Jennifer, and Frank had divorced not too long ago. The marriage hadn't survived, but he and Jennifer wanted to make sure he would still be a part of their daughter's life.

Frank and Emily planned to spend a week together during her summer break. Since the age of six, she had an independent streak, insisting on doing things herself, like learning to tie her shoes or ride a bike. She was twelve now, and growing up fast. Frank was just happy knowing she still wanted to spend time with him, though some days he felt that relating to his daughter was a struggle. The past two days had been wonderful, and he hoped the rest of the week would go as well.

"Baby, lunch is ready," Frank said.

"Dad," Emily started. It wasn't *Daddy* anymore, Frank noted. "I'm not a baby. I'm twelve."

Frank smiled, not wanting to tell her that he would always see her as his baby, and put the plates on the table. They ate in a cozy kitchen, in a small, comfortable house. The inside was warm and inviting, with bright colors and ample lighting from the windows. Not exactly what someone would expect when coming to Frank's home. He'd allowed Jennifer to decorate it after the divorce. She wouldn't allow him to merely exist in a drab house that contained the barest amount of functional furniture.

He sat next to Emily, sharing a casual meal with his daughter. Frank was content. He looked at her, smiling, but something outside caught his eye. A shadow moved across the window. For a moment, Frank questioned if he had seen something.

Please God, not now, he thought, concern flashing across his face.

"What's wrong?" Emily asked.

He smiled and said, "Nothing. Everything's good."

His flashbacks and feelings of paranoia had put stress on his marriage. Frank hadn't coped too well, using anger as a defense, and withdrawing from his family. He had eventually sought help, after the divorce, and was handling everything much better. He wanted things to be perfect with Emily, but he worried about the negative behaviors returning.

It was nothing. You saw nothing, Frank told himself.

He needed this week to work out. For her. He stole a chip from her plate, and she swatted at his hand, laughing. He laughed, but in his mind alarm bells were ringing. Something felt wrong.

He heard a sound outside. Very faint, like a boot scuffing the dirt. But he hadn't heard it, had he? There was no sound. It wasn't at the kitchen door, leading to his backyard. There wouldn't be someone out there, trying to come in and hurt them. Why would there be?

Emily's face was a mirror of the unease he felt and showed. Frank was a statue, his eyes unfocused. She reached for his arm, trying to comfort him, but he moved away. He slid out of his chair with the ease of a shadow and stepped to the counter, pulling a large chef's knife from the wooden block. She was afraid for her father, now.

"Dad? Are you—"

Two sudden booms sounded, nearly simultaneously, as two of the three door hinges exploded. The door smashed inward, and the frame splintered under the boot kicking the entryway open. A man in unmarked olive drab fatigues moved through the entryway before the door fell to the ground, swinging a rifle, an M4 carbine, toward Emily. The barrel seemed to grow as she watched it point in her direction.

The man never saw Frank, who stepped over the fallen door the moment it hit the floor. Frank grabbed the rifle by the barrel, lifting it into the air as he plunged the chef's knife deep into the man's stomach. The intruder screamed in shock and pain.

Frank shouted to his daughter, "Run!"

Another man, just outside the door, lifted the shotgun he had used to blow the door hinges. Frank pulled the barrel of the M4 to one side, spinning the first man around to face the shotgun-wielding intruder. He wrapped one arm around the man's neck and grabbed the grip of the carbine. His human shield didn't put up a fight, more concerned with the knife Frank had left plunged into his belly.

Frank thumbed the selector of the rifle to fully automatic, and fired one-handed, ripping a burst into the shotgunner outside. The deafening boom rattled the windows, as the second intruder fell back into the dirt and crawled out of the line of fire.

Emily was fleeing toward the living room, when she heard the front door smashing open. Another man in the same drab fatigues moved through the doorway. Emily froze in fear, but the burst fire from the kitchen caused the man in the living room to hesitate for a moment and jolted her back into action.

Frank had to get his daughter to safety. He wrenched his human shield's head to one side, snapping the man's neck. He didn't have time to unsling the rifle, so he tossed the dead man aside before rushing to his daughter.

Emily moved down the hall, and Frank crossed through the living room to follow. Shots rang out from the front door, and rounds crashed into the walls around him. One bullet punched into his thigh, almost knocking him over. Another hit him in the ribs and grazed his back. Frank's vision tunneled into blackness for an instant before returning.

He caught up to Emily and used his massive bulk to shield her as they ran toward the garage door. He glanced down at his thigh, and even though the pain was excruciating, he saw no blood. Not even a hole in his jeans. They were using rubber bullets. They wanted him alive. Why?

He opened the door into the garage and led his daughter to the black Ford F-350 parked inside. She opened the passenger door and jumped into the truck. Frank went to his tool shelves and opened a hidden compartment in the wall. He pulled out a Beretta M9 and two spare magazines. Pressing the slide of the weapon back slightly, Frank visually confirmed that there was a round in the chamber. He tucked the magazines into one of his back pockets and hopped into the driver side.

"Buckle up, baby. Keep your head down," he said.

Emily was scared, tears welling up in her eyes. He tried his best to calm her with a smile. Frank usually kept the key inside the truck, for emergency escape purposes. The irony that it was a behavior meant to ease his feelings of paranoia was not lost on him. He pressed the start button, and the powerful V8 diesel engine growled to life.

The doorway connecting the house to the garage burst open, as one man snapped his rifle up and began firing. Franks slammed the gear into reverse and stepped on the gas. Rubber riot rounds were slamming into the windshield, causing spiderweb cracks, as the F-350's wheels spun in place for a moment.

They finally gained traction, and 3 tons of steel and rubber shot backward through the closed garage exterior door. The thin steel door gave only the slightest protest, before it tore free from its rails and rolled under the heavy duty tires.

Looking back over his shoulder, Frank saw a van at the bottom of his driveway. It was parked sideways as a roadblock, to discourage any attempted escape from the garage. The men in the van were not expecting this situation at all. Frank pressed the accelerator down as the pickup truck roared. The van driver's eyes shot open wide, and he began grabbing and pushing random things on the dashboard, completely forgetting how to drive at that moment. Frank swerved the rear of the truck to one side the instant it slammed into the side of the van, nearly tipping it over.

His driver's side window now faced the house, and he saw two more men outside his front door. They lifted their rifles to take aim. Frank put the Ford's gear into drive and reached out with the M9 pistol in his left hand. He emptied a full magazine of 9mm hollow points at the two as he drove away, hitting one of them in the chest before he could fire at the truck.

Pulling away from the area, Frank glanced into the rear view mirror. He saw a car that had been parked across the street from the house speed after him. The van was circling to follow them, as the remaining armed men rushed to get inside it.

Frank lived in a remote area, so he knew the police response time would be much longer than they could afford to wait. Still, he told Emily to call 911 and let them know what was happening. Frank switched the pistol to his right hand and reached into his back pocket with his left for one of the spare magazines. His right forearm was keeping the steering wheel stable, as he thumbed the release that dropped the empty magazine free. He reloaded the M9 and stored it in a holster between his seat and the center console.

The road ahead came to a sharp right turn, and Frank prepared to take the corner without slowing down. Emily had her cell phone out of her pocket, ready to dial emergency services when she caught a glint from something stretched across the road. She yelled for her father to slow down. Frank saw the spike strip right as his daughter shouted a warning.

He swerved the truck to the left, to widen his turn and evade the spikes. The Ford slid off the left side of the road onto the narrow shoulder, and he fought to keep it away from the steep downhill drop into the wooded area. The truck's wheelbase was just too broad, and one of the rear double tires rolled over the spikes and burst. The four-wheel-drive monster slid off the shoulder of the road and nearly tipped over. Frank corrected the wheel, steering off the road to keep them from flipping, but the left-front end crashed into a tree.

The impact caused the big Ford to spin counterclockwise, and the airbags exploded open. A moment later, the rear tire struck something solid during the fishtail spin. Frank and Emily were jerked violently to the right and suddenly felt weightless, as the momentum caused the truck to begin tumbling sideways down the hill. Windows shattered, throwing pebbles of safety glass everywhere. The remains of the black F-350 rocked to a stop deeper in the wooded area.

Frank was dazed, but his body sprang into action, unlatching his seatbelt. The vehicle's driver's side was resting on the ground, and Emily dangled from her seatbelt down toward Frank. She was awake but clutched her right arm with a pained expression.

"Are you okay, sweetheart?" Frank asked.

"I think my wrist is broken," she said.

The shake in her voice and tears in her eyes told Frank that she was trying to be brave for her father.

"We have to keep moving," he said.

Frank released Emily's seatbelt while he cradled her in his arms. He let her down gently, pulled the Beretta from its holster, and tucked it into his pants.

Reaching under the driver's seat, he unfastened an old Mossberg 500 pump-action shotgun that he kept there. It had been his father's gun, and it was older than Frank. He kept the 12-gauge shotgun for more than sentimental reasons. The barrel was shortened, for portability, and he knew that when he pulled the trigger, the old pump gun would not disappoint him. He racked the slide, loading a 00-buckshot shell into the chamber.

"Can you run?" Frank asked.

She clutched her wrist to her chest and gave a small nod.

"You're so brave, and Daddy's very proud of you. I'll get you out of here," he said, kissing her forehead.

Frank stepped out through the shattered remains of the front windshield and visually scanned the area. The car and the van were getting closer, but he saw a man moving across the street with a rifle aimed toward his truck. *That must be the one who set up the spikes,* Frank thought.

The man saw Frank and snapped a quick shot, hitting the truck inches from his face. Frank stepped away from the pickup in a flash, firing his shotgun one-handed while his other arm guided Emily safely behind him. The Mossberg roared, and nine 32-caliber pellets smashed through the rifleman's chest and neck, throwing him to the ground.

The smell of gasoline became apparent in the air, mixed with traces of smoke. Frank turned and scooped Emily into his arms, sprinting deeper into the woods. *I have to get her away before—*

The deafening explosion of his truck was sudden, and the blast carried him off his feet. Frank used his large body to shield his daughter from the heat and shrapnel. He hit the ground hard, and rolled with the impact to keep Emily from getting injured any more. Pieces of burning debris showered down nearby as he lifted his girl to her feet.

"Run!" he told her, dragging himself back up.

A car pulled off to the side of the road, keeping its distance from the burning wreck. Two men exited the rear of the vehicle and covered the truck with their M4 carbines. One of them caught the movement in the woods and spotted Frank and Emily trying to get away.

"Target in the woods!" the man called out, pointing in Frank's direction.

The van then arrived and bounded carelessly down the grassy slope, stopping just beyond the destroyed F-350. The three remaining men from the assault team poured out of the back, moving through the woods at a near run.

Frank heard their pursuers closing in. Emily tried to run as fast as she could, but every jarring step caused agony in her wrist. Tears streamed down her face as she moved. He had to slow the men down.

"Keep going!" Frank yelled.

He spun around and took cover behind a tree. Three men moved in his direction. He racked in a fresh 12-gauge shell, brought the shotgun up and fired. At thirty yards, the buckshot spread, but the hit was still enough to stop one of the pursuers. The other two men crouched and took cover. They tried leaning out to shoot, but Frank kept them suppressed, firing three more blasts, working the pump-action smoothly between shots. He turned and ran back toward his daughter. The air cracked and whizzed around him as the rifles sent more riot rounds in his direction. Pain exploded across his right arm, causing him to drop the Mossberg.

Frank stumbled as he ran, the momentum carrying him forward. He rolled over his shoulder, and came up to a knee, facing the men with rifles. He pulled the Beretta from his waist, put the front sight of the M9 on one of the soldiers, and pressed the trigger twice. At the same moment, the man returned fire with his M4.

Frank's first 9mm round drilled through the man's sternum, where he'd put the front sight. A rubber bullet blasted him high in the chest, near his left shoulder, causing Frank's second shot to miss. The pain overloaded his senses. Frank had to fight to remain conscious. He sat back on the ground, firing the Beretta one-handed.

The slide locked back when the gun was empty, and he was reaching back for his last magazine when something hissed through the air and snapped his head backward. The bright flash of pain in his head turned to a dull ache, and everything became blurry then went black.

* * *

A man in a gaudy, shiny shirt stepped out of the passenger side of the dark sedan parked near the burning truck. The button-up shirt was a fiery red, that sparkled like flames in the sunlight. Only the lower three buttons were closed, allowing the shirt to flow open and show the white tank top and brown leather shoulder holster under it.

He rolled up the sleeves to his elbows while he walked into the woods, listening to the sound of someone screaming. Two men were pulling a young girl toward the van. She was fighting with them while shouting and crying.

Karl Lawler looked back as they walked past, but his white leather shoes never broke their stride toward the injured man lying on the ground. The man on the ground called out to the girl. He turned his attention to Karl and his men, yelling curses and threats between his labored breaths. Karl stopped in front of the man, and looked down at him, with amusement.

Frank Colt was this man's name. *He is highly skilled, and will be dangerous,* the report read. Karl was impressed at how skilled Frank Colt had proved to be, but ultimately, he was confident they would accomplish the mission.

"Please," Frank was pleading, now. "Just let her go. Let her go, and I'll do what you want."

Karl's smile grew as he took his mirror aviator sunglasses off and slid them into his shirt pocket. He reached a hand into his open shirt, and came out with a chrome-plated Desert Eagle, chambered in .44 Magnum. He pointed the muzzle of the monstrous handgun at Frank.

"My friend," Karl said. "we don't want you at all."

Frank looked at his daughter and suddenly realized she was the one they were after. The riot rounds had been used to make sure she would be taken alive.

Karl pulled the heavy trigger and shot Frank in the chest. He flattened back to the ground and gurgled out a final breath. His eyes stayed open. A scream sounded from the van, the girl understanding the meaning of the gunshot. Karl kept the Desert Eagle aimed at Frank's body. *Confirm that Frank Colt is deceased*, the report also said. He fired seven more times into the body, until the gun ran empty. The smile never left Karl's face. He put the pistol back into his shoulder holster, reached into his pocket, and retrieved his sunglasses. Before he left, Karl saw a drop of red on one of his white shoes. He swiped his foot on the dead man's pants to wipe away the blood.

Karl twirled one finger in the air, as a signal for everyone to move out, and walked casually back to his car. The men loaded their fallen into the van, and the two vehicles sped away.

The Hard Kill

The Manning Brothers

CHAPTER

2

DAY 1   15:04 Mountain Time

The phone was ringing when Jennifer came in from her garage. Her daughter, Emily, usually called later in the evening to tell her how her day was. The call was a little earlier than she expected. *Maybe it's just a solicitor,* she thought, but hurried just in case.

She ran to the phone, high heels clicking on the tile floor, trying to pick up before the answering machine did.

"Hello?" Jennifer answered with an expectant smile, reaching down to take off her shoes.

"Is this Jennifer Dawson?" The voice was polite but felt emotionless.

"Um, yes." The smile gave way to confusion. "Who is thi—"

"Formerly married to Frank Colt?" The voice cut her off.

"Who is this?" Jennifer demanded, fighting the small but growing dread in her stomach.

"Jennifer Dawson," the smooth voice continued as if she had never asked a question, "we have your daughter, Emily, age twelve. Frank Colt is dead."

The shoe fell from her hand. Her heart dropped from her chest. Jennifer choked back a gasping cry, covering her mouth with one hand. With the other trembling, she pressed the phone firmly against her ear, for fear of its falling to the floor.

The voice continued, "If you do exactly what we say, when we say, you will see Emily returned to you, safe and unharmed."

Jennifer felt so small and helpless. She kept her hand over her mouth, afraid to make a noise and miss any details.

"Ms. Dawson, we know you work for IntelliSys, as a senior project manager in the research and development department. We know that your team developed a new type of decryption software—"

"H-how do you know about that?" Jennifer blurted out, immediately regretting it.

"Don't interrupt, Ms. Dawson," the voice said, as calm as a teacher chiding a student.

"We know that your team developed a portable device that can use the new software. What we want

Jennifer, is for you to go to work tomorrow morning, just like any typical day.

"Once inside, you will retrieve the prototype device, and take it out of the building. After that we will contact you with further instructions."

Jennifer stood with her knees locked just to stay upright. The hand, on her mouth before, now grasped the counter for stability. This was a nightmare.

"Allow me to make the situation very clear, for the benefit of you and your daughter," the emotionless voice continued. "Under no circumstances are you to call anyone for help. Do not involve the police or any government agencies. Your daughter's life depends on it."

Someone outside the company had found out about the existence of the device. In a company as large as IntelliSys, the leak could have come from anywhere.

What do I do now? she thought. The voice on the phone was very specific. No police, no one else, or they would kill Emily. She had to go in to work tomorrow, gain access to a technology that was kept locked and guarded, and bring it to people she had never met. If they honored their word, they would give her Emily in exchange for the device.

Except, there was no reason they would have to keep either of them alive. Nothing would stop them from taking the device from her and killing them both.

The voice continued to give her very specific conditions for what they expected of her. Jennifer listened helplessly, hopelessly, as tears streamed freely down her face.

CHAPTER
3

DAY 1   19:15   Mountain Time

"Born in the USA"
  Bruce Springsteen

Early Thursday evening at the Fox Hole Bar was livelier than usual on a weekday. It was near the end of happy hour, and many of the customers started their Friday nights a day early. The inside felt friendly and inviting, without the family-themed franchise atmosphere. The bartender changed the program on the flat-screen behind the bar from the local news to the sports channel.

John Stone was a part owner of the Fox Hole, but he enjoyed working an occasional shift, as it allowed him to see how the business was doing. Also, he liked getting to know the locals who came in for a drink or meal.

Tonight, about a dozen people were patronizing the bar. John knew most of them, but two men he didn't know were near the back of the bar, beginning to raise their voices and get aggressive.

One man was at a table, now standing up. He was nearly 6 feet tall, with the strong hands and arms of a working man. He was yelling something to another man at the bar. The man at the bar drank his beer and raised his voice to shoot angry responses back over his shoulder.

This man was not as tall as the first but made up for the height by carrying more weight. His thick muscles were surrounded in places by a generous layer of fat. His bald head, shaved clean by choice, betrayed a receding hairline visible in the stubble.

The talk had grown louder over the course of the past minute, and now both men stood and closed the distance between them. John made his way out from behind the bar and positioned himself in the middle. He placed a hand on each of their shoulders and kept them apart. His arms were also well-muscled, ending in the equally weathered and worn hands of a blue-collar grinder.

John's barrel-chested build had been developed while he was fighting for the freedom and security of his countrymen as an Army Ranger. Unlike many of the men he had served with, who had allowed themselves to settle into the post military life, letting their hardened bodies smooth over with age and dormancy, John maintained his strength and fitness.

He stood over the two men, outmatching them both in height and physique. John turned his head to face each one as he spoke.

"Gentlemen, I'm not sure what this is about, but perhaps it's something that you can settle in a calmer fashion."

John's tone was even, yet it carried authority. His voice matched his close-cropped brown flat top, piercing eyes, and rugged appearance. His facial expression let them know that he wasn't asking. A thick mustache that covered his top lip separated his chiseled-granite jawline and cheekbones, ending just at the corners of his mouth. His head sat atop a powerful neck that started at his ears and splayed out like a pyramid.

"You're right, man," the shorter, thicker man said, putting his hands up and leaning back just enough to separate John's hand from his shoulder. "We just let things get a bit heated. I'm sorry."

The corners of John's mouth pulled up, in what passed for a smile, and his eyes softened as he nodded his acceptance.

The taller man swatted John's arm away. "Get yer hand off me, old man. Think you can just limp over here and tell us what to do?" He turned to face John, now focusing his ire on the old warrior.

John knew it was the alcohol talking, the "super-soldier serum" in a bottle that made this young man think he was invincible. He found himself cutting through faux bravado like this with his words on an almost weekly basis, but this time it felt as if this kid was spoiling for a fight.

"Hey, listen, fights tend to cost me money and customers when they happen." He took a step forward but kept his voice calm. "And when I lose money and customers, it upsets me, so I can't let that happen. Are we clear?" John dipped his head to lock eyes with the brash drunk, letting him know that he expected only one answer.

"Hey, man, it's cool," the young man said, with a smile that was far less genuine than he thought. He let his hands drop to his sides as his shoulders sagged. With most people, this would seem to be a natural gesture of acceptance, but John could read the intention behind the posture.

Interpreting an enemy's body language was an ability that he developed in battle, and it had kept him alive in all his years of service. The stakes tonight were much lower, but his instinct didn't have an off switch.

Just as he expected, the rowdy drunk jerked back and telegraphed a sucker punch. John tucked his chin, leading with his forehead, and stepped inside the wild arc of the swing.

Instead of the billiard-ball *clack* of a head-to-head collision, there was a dull thunk as John landed a perfectly timed counter headbutt that smashed into the bridge of the attacker's nose, using his momentum against him. Blood splattered from the man's nostrils, painting spotty crimson cones on his shirt as he rocked back. The man staggered on his heels before dropping to the ground on his tailbone. After two slight swaying rotations, he fell back.

Laughing and cheering erupted in the bar. It was rare that John had to dirty his hands to take care of a troublemaker, but when it happened, the regulars knew they were in for a show. And tonight, they had not been disappointed. A few of the cheering patrons passed over small bills, losing their bets on how fast John would clean up the mess.

John knelt down and grabbed a handful of the unconscious man's pant leg and dragged him to the front door. Then he put a massive hand under each of the man's armpits and hoisted him up, shouldering him like a sack of flour. John walked to the bus stop near the front of his bar and deposited the man in the normal "trash pick up spot" for troublemakers in his bar.

He turned, wiping his hands together and then along the fronts of his thighs when he noticed a man leaning near the entrance of the bar. He wore his tie loose in the after-hours fashion, dangling from his opened collar. His suit looked like it had fit him five years and 15 pounds ago but now tugged at his midsection. John recognized him, not by his outfit but by the hardened eyes of a man who had served.

"Mark? Is that you?"

"Yeah, John. Been a long time."

John couldn't help but notice that even though Mark Brenner smiled, he looked exhausted. Like the day had just ground him down into an ashtray. They exchanged a big handshake as John clapped a hand on the man's shoulder. He could still feel the muscles of Mark's arm underneath the layer of insulation a desk job seemed to install on even the hardiest of men.

"What's with the silk noose?" John asked. "And the extra padding?"

"Some of us weren't lucky enough to get into the sanitation field after we served," Mark said, glancing over at the unconscious man at the bus stop. "I took a job with *The Company*, behind a desk."

"The CIA?" John had heard rumors that Mark had ended up working with the spooks, but it was somehow strange having it confirmed.

John's smile beamed, but the luster faded as he noticed that it wasn't exhaustion that he saw in the man's face.

"What's wrong, Mark?"

"It's Frank," Mark said with a sigh. "He was murdered."

John felt a hammer blow hit him in his heart. He put a hand over his eyes pressing his temples with his fingers and thumb. He took two deep breaths to calm down.

"What about Jennifer and Emily?" John asked. Frank had shared custody of his daughter, Emily, with his ex-wife.

"Jennifer's okay. She was at work when this happened."

"Where's Emily? Where is my goddaughter?"

"John, they took her."

"Who? What do you mean *they*?" John's fists tightened. Typically never one to lose his temper, he struggled to contain his fury.

Mark saw John was having trouble coping with the bombshell he had just dropped on his friend. "I've got a file here, with everything we currently know." He handed over a bound envelope, thick with papers and folders stuffed inside. "Let's go back to your office."

* * *

John's office was small, but he kept it clean. All of the paperwork was stored and filed with care. His military discipline didn't allow him to let his workspace fall into disarray and, make his job more difficult. He sat at the desk and opened the envelope Mark had given him.

"I'm not going to waste my breath telling you that I'm not supposed to disclose any of this to you," the CIA pencil pusher said. "I know you would eventually get your hands on it anyway, and I wanted you to know everything."

"You still haven't answered my question, Mark. Who did this?"

"We don't have that information yet. But I can tell you that Emily appeared to be the target."

John straightened up when he heard that. "How do you know that? Why would they want Emily?"

Mark rifled through the stack of papers on John's desk, pulling one out and handing it to him. "This is the forensic account of the crime scene. The attackers used rubber bullets, and the autopsy reports show bruising consistent with the findings."

"And they didn't want to risk killing Emily," John said, finishing Mark's explanation.

"Yes," Mark said. "Once they had her, Frank was shot at point blank range. Multiple gunshot wounds from a .44 caliber handgun."

"Is this about Jennifer?" John asked. He knew Frank's ex-wife worked in the tech industry, and that Emily could possibly be used as leverage to get something from Jennifer.

"We believe so," Mark said. "Her position at a major data security company points in that direction. We also know that her relationship with Frank was still amicable, after the divorce, so there is no reason to think that she is a suspect."

"What did she say when you told her?" John asked.

"No contact has been attempted with her yet. The brass feels that if it is a ransom situation, the men responsible will be monitoring her closely, to make sure she doesn't involve the police." Mark grunted as he pulled one of his legs up over his knee and leaned back in the chair. "I've pulled some strings to put a local police detail on her house. They're rather discreet. The bad guys won't spot them."

"I'll talk to her," John said.

Mark nodded, not wanting to dissuade his friend. He needed the ex- soldier's help in the matter but didn't want to come right out and ask, feeling it would be better if John volunteered.

"You'll keep me in the loop when you find anything out?" John said.

"Of course, John. I'll personally keep you informed."

"I'll do whatever it takes to get Emily back and find out who killed Frank."

CHAPTER
4

DAY 1   20:07 Mountain Time

"For Whom the Bell Tolls"
  Metallica

Footsteps clacked, as waxed alligator-skin Louis Vuitton shoes contacted marble flooring, until the man sporting the $10,000 footwear reached the end of the hallway. Warren Ratcliffe stood in his mansion and looked out at his view over the mountain lake as he finished the conversation on a gemstone-studded mobile phone.

"So she's in? You don't foresee any issue getting her to capitulate?" Ratcliffe ran a thumb and forefinger over his trimmed mustache while the voice on the other end confirmed.

"Excellent." He clapped the flip phone closed into his palm with a forefinger.

He slipped his hand holding the phone into the pocket of his slacks and walked back into his formal living room while opening one more button on his silk shirt. The weather was cool this high up, but the pressure of pulling off such a major accomplishment was getting to him.

Jennifer Dawson was a key member of the team that had developed the *PEST* prototype, a device capable of breaking any digital security encryption, and the plan required her cooperation. Jennifer's daughter, Emily, was sitting on a twin-size mattress set on the floor with her back pressed to a marble column. One arm was in a cast, rivaling what any doctor could manage in a hospital. She had her knees pulled up to her chest, with her nose and mouth tucked behind them.

Ratcliffe felt no pity for the injured girl, but the fact that she had not been brought to him "unharmed" as he had requested, caused him to tighten his jaw. Emily's well-being was critical in getting Jennifer to acquire the prototype device, and bring it to him. The family's state of being beyond that had not yet been decided.

Ratcliffe scanned the room, taking stock of the half-dozen mercenaries in his employ. His most trusted enforcer, Mr. Gordon, was busying himself with a small polishing stone, honing the edge of his large-blade tactical folding knife, blowing unseen dust off the razor-sharp edge.

The dark-skinned man was a mystery to Ratcliffe. He guessed him to be South American, possibly Brazilian, because of his accent. Research into his background had turned up very little, other than his skill set, which was impressive. He didn't even know his enforcer's full name, or if Gordon was even his real last name.

What ultimately mattered more than anything else was that Mr. Gordon was always by his side. Violence was the man's stock-in-trade, but he tempered it with loyalty and professionalism. He was the best in the business and worth every penny.

The other armed men in the room ran the gamut of class and race, but all carried similar arsenals and were under the command of Ratcliffe's top enforcer. Their qualities were as yet untested, but the small army had been assembled in a short amount of time to take advantage of a small window of opportunity. These men were here to pull off the mission passed down from the man up top. His eye caught the girl's cast, and again the man seethed at the sloppiness of this hastily mustered force. Mr. Gordon had his work cut out for him.

Emily raised her head to look around the sparsely furnished room with red eyes. Ratcliffe could see that she still had dried blood caked around one nostril and on her cheek. The overpaid buffoons tested his patience.

"Get her cleaned up," Ratcliffe said to two nearby mercenaries. He pointed them to a guest bathroom down the hall from where he had just come.

The guards were rough getting the girl to her feet, and pulling her down the hall. Not a concern of his, but then one of the hired guns muttered something about "perks" of the job.

"Excuse me?" Warren addressed the men as they passed. "What was that you just said?"

The men exchanged nervous glances. Almost under his breath, one of them said, "I, uh…I said now we get to have a little fun. It's one of the perks of this job."

Ratcliffe's eyes narrowed, boring holes through the mercenary. He looked over at Mr. Gordon and dipped his chin in an almost imperceptible nod. His loyal head of security nodded and slid the folding knife back into the slim pouch on his belt.

The hired goon's eyes lit up in horror as the enforcer brought his knee up to chest height, chambering his leg. In a flash, Mr. Gordon's foot shot out in a picture perfect sidekick. There was a wet crunch as the outer edge of his foot thrust into his target's Adam's apple, pinning the man's head and neck to the marble column behind him.

Mr. Gordon pushed off his support leg, leaning more of his body weight into his extended foot. As he twisted his foot like he was extinguishing a cigarette, the mercenary's broken neck crackled. As smooth as he fired the kick out, Mr. Gordon pulled his foot back, knee still held high, with his shin now vertical. The man's body slumped to the floor as the enforcer wiped a hand down along the outside of his own lower leg, snapping the fabric of his slacks straight before placing the foot back on the ground.

Ratcliffe turned to address the rest of the stunned men in the room.

"Don't let my indifference to the little girl mislead you," he said. "That type of behavior will not be tolerated. We are not monsters."

Mr. Gordon pointed to another pair of mercenaries. "You two clean this mess up." He pointed down at the body on the floor next to him. "Take his gear, and make sure he disappears for good."

* * *

Emily had already closed the bathroom door before the man outside was killed. She knew what happened, and was thankful she'd made it to the bathroom instead of having to watch the gruesome scene. Her hands shook with fear, but her mind switched gears, looking for an opportunity she could exploit.

Emily turned the cold-water faucet on and wet a hand towel to wipe away the dried blood on her face. Fear gripped her, but a small sense of defiance bubbled up. Keeping the water running, she quickly opened all the drawers and cabinets, looking for something, anything, she could use when the opportunity arose.

Her heart sank when she saw that everything was empty. Emily turned off the water and was staring at her reflection when the guard out front pulled her attention back.

"You almost done in there?"

"Just a second," she said, flushing the toilet to buy a few more seconds. The toilet paper roll popped out in her mind. She pulled the roll off the holder and pulled the metallic tube apart, retrieving the spring inside. Emily stuffed it into her pocket and did her best to replace the roll, wadding some toilet paper into the halves of the metal tube so it would stay on the side brackets.

She wiped her palms across her eyes and looked in the mirror again. Confidence and hope almost replaced the crippling fear she had felt when they first brought her here. *Be strong, like Dad taught you.*

CHAPTER

5

DAY 1   20:45 Mountain Time

"Separate Ways"
Journey

"Please be assured that no one will notice us watching over you, ma'am," a tall man with a beard said.

Jennifer nodded. "Thank you, Officer."

"Remember, you can also call us if you need anything," the younger of the two undercover officers said.

With a smile and nod, Jennifer closed the front door, watching through the square glass panel as they returned to their car parked down the street. She still felt helpless, even knowing the police were out there.

She locked the door, walked back to the living room, and picked up the empty wine-glass from the coffee table. She placed a hand over her mouth and closed her eyes, trying to force the sudden tears and sobs back. After a moment she took in a deep breath and exhaled, feeling the shaking recede.

Jennifer composed herself and headed into the kitchen. Her hand brushed the light switch, but a voice in the darkness called out just before she flipped it on.

"Jennifer," the voice said.

It was a soothing and calming tone, but the man behind it was tough and determined. A voice from her past she recognized. She turned the light on, and saw an imposing figure standing next to the kitchen table.

"John," she said, feeling a relief she hadn't felt since Emily was taken.

John Stone was a friend of the family. He'd served with her ex-husband, Frank, as an Army Ranger, and he was Emily's godfather. The two hugged in greeting, and his strong presence was comforting to Jennifer.

"How long have you been there?" she asked.

"Long enough to hear you talking to the police," John said. "I slipped by them because I didn't want to complicate things. Just wanted to check on you, but I also need some information about what's happening."

Jennifer put the glass into the sink and pulled her robe tighter, folding her arms across her abdomen. She nodded and sat down at the table with John.

"I got a call this afternoon. Some man saying he had Emily and he wanted me to steal something for them."

She told John everything she could remember about the call, and about the device that they wanted her to take for them. They needed her security clearance to get to the device since it was still in the prototype stage.

"What is the device? What is it used for?" John asked.

"We've named the prototype PEST," she said. "It's capable of cutting through any known digital security encryption today, and it can learn to defeat anything newer it may come across in a short amount of time."

"PEST?" John asked.

"The man who first created the project initially called it *Pestilence*, because it works sort of like a disease against any encryption it encounters. We shortened the name so that it wouldn't sound so…apocalyptic." A small smile crept onto her face.

"Cyberwar. The war of the future," John said. "Can you tell me anything else about the caller? Any odd speech patterns, like a stutter, or a distinct accent?"

Jennifer's smile grew. "I can do better than that. My home phone is part of my internet service. Any calls that come through it leave a digital signature."

She got up and walked to the counter, where a small laptop sat next to her purse.

"I've been running a trace program to break through what little security the caller on the other end had."

She opened the laptop and logged in, pulling up a document she put together before placing the computer in front of John.

"I traced the call to a cell phone belonging to this man, Karl Lawler."

The document had his name, known address, and a short list of prior convictions. Karl's most recent mugshot occupied the top-right corner of the page, staring out at anyone reading about him.

John smiled as well. The expression looked out of place, like trying to stretch cement. "Clever."

"It took some time, but I was able to isolate his phone's location. I can only get within a few hundred yards or so, but he should be around this intersection right now."

John looked at the map displayed on Jennifer's laptop. A circle spread out covering several buildings in the area. He traced a finger along each, as he mentally drove through the intersection. He pointed at the largest of the buildings.

"He's right there. Ambrosia Nightclub."

Jennifer pulled the SIM card from her phone and slipped another one in, then handed the mobile device to John. "Here, use this to stay in touch with me. I've got another one like it that I'll be using."

John grabbed the phone without questioning and slid it into his coat pocket.

"I can contact you when I get more information," she said. "Also, the phone has a short-range jamming signal built into it. A little something we've been developing in my lab."

"Could come in handy."

"You have to stay close," she said. "It's only good for about three hundred feet or so, but it should prevent any digital signal from broadcasting."

John stood up and placed a hand on Jennifer's shoulder. "I'll find out who's behind this and get Emily back safe."

She put a hand on his and nodded, pressing her lips together and struggling to keep the tears at bay again. She barely noticed John leaving the room.

CHAPTER
6

Emily Colt retrieved the spring from her pocket and started the process of straightening a length of the coiled metal. She had been moved from the wide-open formal living room into a different room, with a lock on the door. The bare mattress had been brought in with her and shoved unceremoniously into the far corner. Like the living room earlier, this new space was also empty.

Before her parents' divorce, Emily's father had grown increasingly paranoid and obsessed with being prepared for worst-case scenarios. During that time, he would regularly teach her random skills that he thought would be necessary to survive in a new broken world.

Her father eventually sought therapy to help him cope with his paranoia and difficulty adjusting to his civilian life. Emily forgot many of the things her father had tried to teach, but learning how to make and use a set of lock picks stuck with her.

Satisfied with the straightened length, she grasped the wire firmly with both hands and worked it back and forth, trying to bend it over and over again. The small, sturdy steel spring dug deep, bruising the flesh of her small fingers, all the way down to the bone. The pain was too much to tolerate, making the task difficult. Anger welled up inside, countering the pain. She needed to push her emotions down, and concentrate.

Footsteps thudded quickly down the hall, and she stopped, stashing the spring underneath the mattress. She listened for a few minutes, too scared to continue. Again the sound of heavy steps could be heard, this time at a slower pace, and accompanied by a lighter set of footfalls, both heading back the way the first man had jogged by. More minutes passed until Emily realized that the only sound she could hear was her own breath, flowing in and out through her nostrils.

With the immediate threat of being discovered now out of her mind, she pulled the corner of the bed up and saw a small gap in the baseboard where it met the floor. Emily fed the straightened portion of the spring in as far as it would go and used the edge of the base board to bend the metal. She had to pull the spring, turn it over, and then feed it back in, to bend it the other way.

With the metal softened, she finished working it back and forth until it finally gave way and snapped.

She repeated the process two more times, just in case she needed different lengths. Emily used the baseboard to bend smaller crimps into one of the bits of spring to form a small "M" shape at the tip.

She now had a set of crudely made lock-picks. The rest of the spring was too short to be of any use, so she ripped a small slit in the mattress and discarded the bits inside. She pocketed her tools and sat back against the wall, planning her next move.

CHAPTER

7

DAY 1   22:58 Mountain Time

"I Wanna Rock"
Twisted Sister

The scene at Ambrosia Nightclub was chaotic at first glance. Bodies packed together on the dance floor moved to the deliberate drum-beats and the growling guitar riffs of classic '80s hair metal bands. Smoke and pulsing laser lights added to the retro atmosphere of the exclusive new club. The deejay's state-of-the-art equipment made her seem out of place, but she controlled the crowd with perfect musical choreography.

Karl Lawler slipped through the crowd to one of the neon-rimmed tables in the VIP area. Distracted by the beautiful bodies dancing around him, he took his time to get to his destination. Karl fired out casual pick-up lines to random women, but over the pounding music, they fell upon practically deaf ears.

He made a mental note of a few of the more beautiful women to keep an eye out for later and continued to swim through the crowd. Making his way to his destination, Karl saw his contact, Trevor, a fat man taking up half the couch with a woman on either side of him.

Trevor wore a white suit jacket and pants over a light pink T-shirt. Rolled up sleeves and loafers with no socks added to the throwback look, and the lines of cocaine he snorted from the mirrored table-top completed the package.

The two women were a clear signal that drugs and power go a long way for a man like Trevor. Karl never enjoyed his meetings with the slob, but he was one of Warren Ratcliffe's best suppliers of hard-to-get weapons and technology.

"K-Dawg! What's going on, my man?" Trevor yelled over the music as he saw him approach.

Karl hated him. Hated his look, his smell, and the way he purposely pronounced *dog*, like it was spelled with an *a* and a *w*, when he called Karl *K-Dog*. Trevor was soft. He wasn't a hardened killer, and Karl hoped for the day the disgusting slug would no longer be of use to Warren. Karl would show him then what it meant to have real power. Until that day, he was forced to keep attending these meetings.

"It's all good, Trev. How are things going in your world?" Karl asked.

"You know me, dawg. It's always ladies' night in my world." Trevor leaned back to put his arms around the women on either side of him. "I'm swimmin' in so much 'tang, I'm like an astronaut!" He let out a laugh that sounded like a garbage disposal full of raw chicken skin, and the women joined in the laughter a second later.

Trevor nodded to the women on either side of him and asked, "You wanna taste, man?"

"Maybe later," Karl said. "Let's get this business done first. Then we can party."

"Excuse us, ladies," Trevor said.

He slid his clammy, pale hands down the back of each woman and squeezed their gorgeous curves between his bloated fingers. They needed no other encouragement to be away from him as they stood to leave the VIP area. One of the women grabbed the vial of cocaine from the table as they walked off.

* * *

John Stone stepped through the doors of Ambrosia and swept his gaze across the crowded

51

nightclub, looking for Karl. He wore a polo shirt and dark pants, the outfit of a bartender. It was enough to satisfy the dress code, but he appeared underdressed compared to most of the other club-goers. John also carried a Colt 1911 semiautomatic pistol, chambered in .45 caliber. It was tucked into a holster inside his waistband, allowing him some measure of concealment with his shirt covering it. The 1911 was typically not a weapon carried concealed, due to its size, but John's large frame allowed him to pull it off successfully.

The phone's screen cast a blue glow as John glanced at the photo of Karl. He worked his way around the perimeter of the club. It was still crowded on the edges, but not like the dance floor with its mass of bodies. John's eyes scanned everyone quickly looking for his target, a skill from his military days to quickly assess any potential threats.

As he moved around, John also tried to pick Karl out from the dance floor. He made his way deeper into the club, and the VIP area came into view. He worked his way in that direction as he pushed through the crowd.

He spotted Karl at a table, talking to a fat, sweating man in a white suit. Karl stood to leave and made his way onto the dance floor. John took a moment to consider the man in the VIP area as a possible person of interest in finding the ones who had taken Emily. He would have to think about that later. He already knew Karl Lawler was involved, so Karl was at the top of John's list.

John made his way to the middle of the club, attempting to intercept Karl before he got too deep into the mob of dancers. He was nearly on his target when a woman carrying a tray full of oddly shaped glasses filled with different colored liquids, nearly collided with him. John stopped to make sure she didn't spill anything, and let her pass. When he looked back to the dance floor, Karl was already well into the crowd.

John tried to work his way toward him, but the mass of bodies was difficult for a man his size to wade through without causing a scene. He saw his target, near the middle of the floor now, trying to talk with some women over the pounding music.

He reached Karl but stepped past him while twisting in time with the beat. As John turned, he whipped the back of his fist into Karl's face quickly. His knuckles snapped into his target's temple. John used the shift of his hips to both generate power and disguise the strike as an awkward dance move.

Karl was stunned right out of his conversation with the beautiful woman dancing next to him. His legs buckled, but John was already helping him up and apologizing for the accident. He pulled one of Karl's arms over his massive shoulders and helped to walk him off the floor as he would a friend who'd had one too many drinks.

They'd made it to the edge of the dance floor when Karl regained enough of his sense to realize he was being escorted out by someone he didn't know.

"Hey, man, wuzzat? Get off me, man. Who are you?" he said to the mustachioed mountain.

John laughed it off like he was talking to a friend. "It's cool. I got you. We're just going out for a little fresh air," he said, carrying him to the exit.

Karl got more aggressive as he pulled away, yelling, "Get your hands off me, man! I'll kill you!"

John tried to stay calm and friendly, but he noticed a bouncer near the front watching the two of them now. He grabbed his target in as friendly a headlock as he could and continued to the front entrance.

Karl panicked, flailing and screaming to jerk his body away. John kept his demeanor friendly but held the vise grip around his head. It was clear now that they weren't going to get out without trouble. Another bouncer joined the first one at the front entrance, as they made their way toward him.

"I'm not trying to cause any trouble. We were just heading out right now," John said.

He wasn't going to fool them into thinking Karl was his friend, so John tried to take a common-sense approach. If the bouncers let them leave, there would be no disruption in the club, but these two didn't buy it.

"Let him go. Right now," the first bouncer said to John.

His posture was menacing, and his partner stepped to the side, blocking their path out. The body language was all meant to intimidate. It didn't come close, but John played along. He felt these two were looking forward to the situation's getting physical. If it came to that, it would be best for John to have both hands free.

He released his grip, and Karl fell to the floor, spitting blood and cursing at his captor. He bolted between the bouncers and toward the exit in a flash. John moved to stop him, but the bouncers took the move as aggressive and attacked.

Fighting two on one is difficult. Even more so in a closed or crowded space, but it was clear to John that these two spent more time looking like fighters than being them.

The first one stepped in and threw a ponderous haymaker with all of his momentum behind it. John stepped with ease to the side of the punch and lifted a foot to trip the bouncer.

The second man's attack surprised John. Not because the punch caught him off guard, but because the bouncer threw the same giant right hand as his buddy had. This time, John stepped inside the big arcing punch and lifted his left arm to protect his head while driving his elbow into the man's face. The forward momentum caused the point of John's elbow to collide with the bouncer's chin. The bouncer's head snapped up, sending him crashing to the floor.

John looked up to see Karl pushing the front door open. He started after him, but two beefy arms wrapped around his body, pinning his arms to his sides. Distracted by Karl's escape, John hadn't noticed a third man joining the fight.

He was lifted off his feet and turned back around. The first bouncer was back on is feet. The arms were iron bars wrapped around his body, holding him in place. The bouncer standing in front of him measured off another big right hand.

John snapped his head back, smashing his captor's nose, and timed the other man's punch for a counter. He bent forward at the waist, pulling the third bouncer forward. John ducked under the fist as it connected with the forehead of the man holding him. There was a sickening crack as the bones in the attacker's hand crumbled under the pressure of the punch meeting thick skull.

The first bouncer howled in agony as the third man fell backward, like a giant tree that had been cut down. John turned to make his way toward the exit before anyone else could slow him down. Karl was outside the effective radius of Jennifer's jamming device. John had to find him fast.

CHAPTER

8

DAY 1   23:40 Mountain Time

"Panama"
Van Halen

Karl burst outside through the door of the club. *Who was that lumberjack trying to get me out here?* he wondered. He paused for a moment, trying to remember where he had parked his car. Karl turned left and sprinted around the building, down the side alley to the parking lot, fumbling for his keys.

He spotted his car parked away from the building and cursed himself for being so vain, refusing to park it too close to other cars or people. A laughing couple stepped out from behind a dark sedan, crossing his path. Karl tried to shove between them, but they all collapsed in a pile.

"What the hell?!" the man yelled, on his back. The woman with him crashed into the front of their car and rolled off the hood with a pained, angry scream. Karl pushed off the ground to keep moving and realized he had lost his keys. He was frantic, scanning the lot before he found them peeking out from under the woman's purse. Karl grabbed the bag to toss it aside.

The woman grabbed his arm to pull him away. "That's my purse, you pathetic—"

Karl spun and punched her full in the face. She let out a yelp and collapsed. The man stood and rushed him. The two of them collided and stumbled back to the ground, as the man flailed with wild punches down on Karl's head and arms. Karl shoved the man away while reaching under his jacket to pull the chrome Desert Eagle from his shoulder holster. The man's eye's shot wide open, and he held his hands up while scooting away with his hands and elbows. Karl rolled away, swiped his car keys off the ground, and sprinted for his vehicle.

He finally reached his metallic red V10 Audi R8 Spyder and pressed the button on his fob to unlock the door. The car growled to life almost as soon as Karl settled into the seat. He backed out of his space, nearly swiping the car next to him, and threw the car into drive.

Karl maneuvered the Audi into the back alleyway to get it out onto the street. He was fishing a phone out of his pocket when he saw the giant from the club running toward him.

* * *

John exited the club and saw no sign of his target. He glanced left and right, then cursed under his breath. He was about to guess which direction to move in when he heard shouting from behind the building.

It wasn't a guarantee he would find Karl there, but his instinct told him to act on it. John ran to the left and rounded the corner. He saw an alleyway that led to a second parking lot behind the club. He had to get there before Karl got into his car and drove away.

John sprinted as fast as he could down the alley and heard the growling engine of a car heading straight for him. *Was this the only way out?* Then he saw the small red car roaring at him.

Even in the moonlight, he could see Karl behind the windshield. The man had a devilish grin, as he gripped the wheel, expecting to win this mismatched game of chicken. The Audi Spyder screamed toward John. His 1911 pistol would not be an option here. The parking lot was behind Karl, and John couldn't be sure that there wouldn't be bystanders in the line of fire.

John looked for anything that could be used to stop him or slow him down. A steel dumpster against the wall was all he could find. Reaching it before Karl would be challenging, and the distance got shorter with every passing second. John lunged with steel-piston strides and reached the big metal box with just enough time to yank it away from the wall and into the path of the car.

The dumpster now blocked most of the alley, forcing Karl to brake and swerve his car to avoid a collision. The Audi screeched as it scraped its passenger side along the steel container. Karl jerked the wheel back to the right, causing the rear end to slam into the wall of the next building, losing some of his speed.

John leaped onto the car as it tried to get away, and dug his fingers around the lip of the hood. He smashed a fist into the windshield, aiming for Karl's face. The impact buckled the laminated glass and created a spiderweb of cracks radiating out, blocking the driver's view.

Karl was in a full panic now, screaming while dropping his phone and reaching for his pistol. He jammed the muzzle forward and jerked the trigger. A large hole exploded through the glass, and John ducked to avoid the shot. He rolled his body up the windshield to the roof and flattened out, grabbing either side for support. John searched out the spots where the beastly convertible's top connected to the vehicle.

Karl was momentarily dazed from the loud report and muzzle flash, but he regained control and finally turned onto the street as he saw John roll up to the top of his car. He aimed his gun upward and fired two more times, bracing for the blast by shutting his eyes momentarily.

The shots came dangerously close to hitting John. He found the roof's connection points and grabbed the passenger-side edge with a large hand. John tore the joint free with a grunt of effort and peeled the convertible top open like a can of sardines.

He was met with a hysterical scream and a wildly swinging hand shoving a shiny Desert Eagle through the opening. Karl tried to get the gun as close as possible so that he couldn't miss. John grabbed the weapon as his hand swallowed Karl's. He squeezed and twisted with all his might. Parts of the handgun, as well as the hand holding it, gave in and broke under the pressure.

Karl's mind was overloaded with fear and pain, and he felt the small bones in his hand crumble. He just wanted to jump out and run away. They sped toward a red light at an intersection. Karl tried to make it through, but a truck crossed right in front of him.

He stomped on the brake and swerved to the right, sideswiping the other vehicle. The impact of the collision launched John off the top of the Audi. He landed hard on the street, rolling with the momentum. Brakes screeched as drivers desperately tried not to hit him.

John stood up on wobbly legs. He saw the tires of the convertible spin up clouds of smoke, then break away. The driver of the truck got out. He was a gangly bearded man with the area around his gray facial hair stained a golden brown, like his teeth. The man adjusted his hat sporting a beer logo on the front and walked over to John, plucking a cell phone from his faded jeans.

"Are you okay, man?" he asked. Then he added, "Were you on top of that car?"

John grabbed the man by his shirt, to add seriousness to his tone when he spoke but also to steady himself.

"Sir, I need to borrow your truck," he said. He released his grip and headed for the old pick-up.

"Just wait a minute," the man said, putting a hand on John's shoulder. "You can't just take—"

A solid fist caught the driver completely off guard. It slammed into his stomach, stealing the breath from his lungs. The truck driver dropped to his hands and knees, struggling for air while his nervous system rebooted.

John climbed into the old brown-and-white pickup and started the engine. He threw the loose stick shift into first gear and slammed his foot down on the gas. The truck lurched, and the tires sprayed loose asphalt out before finally gaining some traction. Karl's Audi grew smaller as John took off toward him.

* * *

Karl pushed the Spyder as fast as it would go. His car sported a beefy V10 engine, but a damaged axle prevented him from exploiting its full power.

Who is that guy? Is this about the girl and her mom? If that was true, Karl had to let Warren know about the situation. His cell phone sat next to his gun in the passenger seat, sliding as he weaved through traffic. Karl reached for the phone, cursing as his broken fingers protested. The device nearly fell under the seat, but he managed to barely hold on with his damaged right hand.

He checked the rearview mirror to make sure the stranger wasn't following. When it was clear, Karl turned his attention to the phone in his hand, but his peripheral vision caught something in the mirror. A big pickup truck was approaching fast, passing other cars as it closed the distance. It was still a ways back, but it was gaining with every weave through the traffic.

Karl scanned the area, searching for a way to evade his pursuer. He spotted a small side street between two buildings and smashed his foot on the brake. He struggled to make the sharp right turn using only one hand to steer, but he managed to maneuver the Audi around the corner, scraping a fender against a parked car. The side street was narrow, and he slowed a bit so he could concentrate on making a phone call.

Karl spotted a stop sign at the end of the small street, leading out onto the main road ahead. Blaring his horn, Karl burst from the alley, trying to take the left turn onto the street as fast as he could. The red Spyder shot out, horn blaring, skidding to start a wide turn.

He managed to get back onto the main road without another accident. With his good hand holding his phone, he didn't have full control of the steering wheel, so Karl kept his speed lower than he would have liked. The call went through and the other phone began to ring, then the call suddenly failed and ended. He cursed and stuffed the phone into his shirt pocket.

He never saw the brown-and-white truck pull up beside him. The driver sideswiped into the right side of his Audi, catching him completely unaware and sending the small red car careening to the side.

***

John darted in and out of traffic with his borrowed truck, shortening the distance to the Audi. *Borrowed*, he thought, knowing it was a lie. He had stolen the man's truck, and though he would be more than willing to return it, John knew that didn't make it any less of a crime. He justified his actions by telling himself that this was to save a young girl, and that losing his target would put her in even more danger than she was already in.

He was closing the distance when the little red sports car turned down a side street. John guided the truck onto a wide road that ran parallel to the narrow path. His phone was running the jammer, and he hoped he could close the distance before Karl could send a call out.

John was on the red Spyder moments after it emerged from the side street. His first sideswipe almost took the car completely out of action. Just as his target was regaining control, John swerved his steering wheel, smashing the truck into Karl's car again. The little convertible was sent nearly into the oncoming traffic in the next lane, and John pushed the accelerator down, preparing for another hit. As he drew near, Karl sped away, his engine able to pull the smaller car away faster than the large truck could keep up.

* * *

Karl glanced over at his passenger seat and saw that the gun was no longer there. He frantically searched the floor of the car and saw it bouncing around near the brake pedal. He let his foot off the accelerator for an instant so he could reach the pistol and quickly sat back up, scanning his rear-view mirror.

In the cracked shards of his side mirror, he saw the pickup truck moving up on the right side. Karl couldn't hold the pistol effectively with his damaged right hand, so he gripped it with his left and fired across his body.

The bullet ricocheted off the hood, and the truck kept back far enough to keep Karl from being able to aim at the driver directly. The truck faded back a little, then suddenly jerked in his direction, hitting the

Audi with a solid strike to the rear fender. The sports car swerved into a fishtail, then overcorrected, driving through a fence into a construction site for a new building.

On the loose dirt and uneven terrain, the truck would have more of an advantage. Karl cursed. He had to get out of here and back on the street. The roar of the pickup's engine grew louder as he made several random turns between portable structures and large vehicles. He gunned the engine and drove down a worn path that led back to the road, watching the light fence getting closer to him.

The monstrous truck abruptly cut off his only path of escape, skidding in front of his car, sending out a rooster tail of rocks and debris. The cloud of dirt and dust spread out in a plume as his pursuer barreled straight for him.

Karl screamed, stuck his arm out the window, and emptied his pistol at the oncoming truck. He prayed the shots would be enough to get the other man to swerve. The truck continued to accelerate straight toward him, the driver not even flinching, as two of the bullets smashed through the truck's windshield.

Karl's car wiggled indecisively as he panicked, choosing a direction in which to get off the path and dodge the oncoming vehicle. The Spyder almost squeezed out of the way, but Karl felt the truck smash along the side his car, and knock him off course again. Petrified of the man in the truck, he kept the gas pedal pinned all the way down with his foot. He tried to point his car toward the main road and oversteered, sending the car bounding in the direction of a bulldozer.

In a last-ditch effort to avoid a collision, Karl went with the skid, hoping to make it around the massive construction vehicle. The blade of the bulldozer gouged into the car's body just behind the front-left fender, shearing the door from its hinges and tearing the rear wheel from the axle. The impact stopped the small car dead in its tracks.

* * *

John stopped the truck close by and stepped out with his pistol drawn. He closed the distance with smooth steps, keeping his aim on the slumped figure in the driver's seat. Looking through the passenger side, John saw that one of Karl's arms had been severed by the crash. Arterial pulses of blood gushed from the ripped, jagged wound.

He reached the driver's side and saw Karl moving his mouth, wordlessly pleading as he bled out. He eventually stopped moving, and his eyes stayed fixed and open. John pulled out a small flashlight and examined the inside of the wreck, finding the remains of Karl's phone. He cracked the body open to retrieve the SIM card inside, dropping it into his shirt pocket before calling Jennifer.

After only one ring, he heard her answer, "Hello?"

"It's me," John said.

"Are you okay?" Jennifer asked. She had been following Karl's movement on her laptop.

"I'm fine, but Karl's a dead end. I have the SIM card to his phone. Maybe you can find something useful on it."

"That's good," she said, then asked, "What happened to Karl?"

"He was caught dozing behind the wheel," John replied.

The sound of police sirens grew as the officers followed the not-so-subtle trail to the construction site.

"I'll call you later," John said, as he left the scene on foot, using shadows for concealment.

CHAPTER

9

DAY 2   00:01   Mountain Time

Warren Ratcliffe leaned forward in the high-back leather chair, placing his palms on the dark hardwood table in his conference room. The pair of 70-inch OLED displays curved around to form an arc at the head of the table, showing him the other participants in the video conference. Even though half a dozen smaller windows split the image, each showing someone on the other end, only three of them had recognizable faces staring back. The other three were either silhouettes or some type of digitally altered signal to mask the faces and voices of the participants.

"As I mentioned at the beginning of this meeting, I assure you that our asset is making progress in acquiring the prototype for us," Ratcliffe said. He had the urge to wipe away an imagined droplet of sweat on his brow, but he feared the gesture would be a sign of weakness to the others.

"You can assure us that the asset is fully cooperative, I hope," one of the digitally altered attendees said.

"Of course. I've taken steps to ensure that Ms. Dawson will have no choice but to do what we ask of her."

"And what does this device do again?" This question came from a heavyset man in the lower left window. His head was shaved clean, showing a pattern of traditional tribal tattoos in a crescent arc on the left side of his head, tucking beneath the collar of his silk burgundy shirt. The man had a long, wispy beard of mostly gray hairs wiggling their way down his chin, almost covering the knot of his tie.

Warren crafted a response in his head that didn't sound like he was repeating himself once again. "In simple terms, it's a decryption device. It uses a sophisticated, layered algorithm to entangle itself in a secure system, forcing the encryption to, for lack of a better phrase, burst at the seams."

"How does it accomplish that?" the big Pacific Islander asked.

Warren was starting to lose his patience with this group of distracted mental munchkins. "Again, it is a self-replicating set of instructions, all working in concert with the host. It overwhelms all known digital encryption, including government security protocols, and passes all the data back along to the host."

"Right, and what good is this device if you've got to break in and get the information even to use it?" the pale, waxy faced cadaver in the lower center window chimed in. "And how much information are you talking about. Megabytes? Terabytes?"

"I don't think you're grasping the scope of what this device can manage."

"Don't presume to tell us what we can and cannot grasp, Ratcliffe." The digital warbling voice of the silhouetted man in the top center rattled in his speakers. The man leaned forward when he spoke, clearly upset.

Warren dipped his head low, looking up at the people on the screen. "My apologies, sir. I meant no offense."

When the intimidating shadow receded, Warren continued. "This device has incredible potential. It is capable of infecting entire networks if it has access. You ask how much data we're talking about? It is capable of slicing through exabytes of data in minutes. The amount of data we could secure will make Wikipedia look like a drop of water in a sea of information."

"I'm not sure you've answered my original question," the waxen man said. "You boast about your ability to crack even the most elaborate encryption like a walnut, yet you don't have any files, nor the device to accomplish what you claim."

The statement set the others off, with one or two trying to defend Ratcliffe's position while the rest shouted over one another.

Jackals, bickering over rotted scraps, Warren thought.

"Gentlemen, please. I don't wish for this meeting to devolve into shouting and chest thumping. Would it put your minds at ease if I told you that I am in the process of recruiting a team of high-level hackers?"

The arguing slowed as the men returned their attention to Warren.

"For your sake, I hope you find the best people for the job," the shadow in the top center said.

"Also, I would hate to see you fail in your task to get your hands on the device," the man in the upper left said.

"Of that, I have no doubt," Warren said. "We've got an insurance policy to make sure the woman tasked with the mission cooperates. We've got her daughter."

The body language of the men in the video conference suggested that the answer was satisfactory, except for the fat tattooed man. Warren wasn't sure if he didn't like the plan or the fact that they'd kidnapped a young girl to pull it off. He didn't care what the blubbery oaf thought anyway.

With the barest acknowledgment, each of the men bowed out of the meeting, killing their feeds.

Warren stood and straightened his suit jacket before stepping out of the conference room in his mansion. He turned to the man outside guarding the door.

"Tell Mr. Gordon I need to talk to him."

"Of course, sir." The guard pressed a finger to his earpiece and keyed his mic to send the order to someone who could pass along the message.

Those idiots at the top had no idea what Warren and the device were capable of doing. He entertained the thought of collapsing the entire power structure and taking over when a knock sounded on the massive oak doors.

"Come in, Mr. Gordon."

CHAPTER

10

DAY 2 01:30 Mountain Time

John walked through an apartment complex parking lot a few blocks away from the construction site where he had left Karl and the stolen pickup truck. He called Jennifer back, once he knew he was safe.

"The phone I gave to you has an extra SIM card slot," Jennifer said. "Put his card in there, and I should be able to access the information on it from here."

He found the slot after a short search and inserted the card.

"Okay, it's in there."

"Alright, give me a second to access it."

"Take your time," he said. "I need a few moments myself."

He needed another vehicle so he could move quickly to investigate any clues Jennifer might find on Karl's SIM card.

The parking lot was full at this time of night, so he had the luxury of finding a suitable vehicle. Power and performance were low on his list. He needed a car that would be easy to break into and get started. John walked as casually as he could through the parking lot, holding the phone to his ear, and finally found the car he would choose.

Jennifer was speaking again.

"John, I'm looking through his recent calls and message history. I see a few calls and texts sent to one particular number over the last two days."

John held the phone between his shoulder and ear as he approached the driver's side door of a silver late-model Nissan Sentra.

Jennifer continued, "The number belongs to Ivan Ferrier. I pulled the text messages between them, and it sounds like Ivan will be meeting someone at a warehouse just off Sixth Street, near the river. I don't know what the meeting is going to be about, but it looks like it's going to be in a few hours."

John spoke to Jennifer as he worked to open the car door. "I don't even know how you're getting this information from just that little card," he said.

"You'd be shocked to know what kind of personal info I can get just from your phone," Jennifer said.

With a slight shake of his head, he said, "Maybe I shouldn't know. I'd better get going. Send me any information you can find out about Ferrier."

He ended the call and stuffed the phone into his pocket. Besides his Colt 1911 semiautomatic, he was carrying a small bag that fit into his front pocket, with a few emergency-survival-type items in it. Using a simple technique, and a couple of the little tools from the bag, John unlocked the door quietly and slipped into the front seat. A few moments later, he started the car and backed out of the parking space.

He drove slowly out of the apartment complex to avoid suspicion, and merged the nondescript silver sedan into traffic, toward his next location.

CHAPTER

11

"Shoot to Thrill"
AC/DC

John pulled over in the Sentra across the street from a warehouse-type building. It was the location of the meeting, so he needed to approach as quietly as he could. He didn't have a picture of his target, so he had to watch how everyone interacted with one another.

He decided to park his car out of sight and watch from inside it until he knew who was coming. A quick visual search of the area found it empty, except for a few white vans and trucks in the fenced-in lot. They were company vehicles parked there overnight.

An hour and a half into John's surveillance, a lone Mercedes sedan arrived and parked near the meeting location. Two men stepped out of the car. Both were pretty well-dressed, but one of them was clearly in charge. They scanned the area quickly and seemed confident they were alone.

It appeared to John that they had arrived early to the meeting to make sure things would be clear. Or maybe they wanted to set up an ambush. *These guys have some real trust issues,* John thought. He needed to find out if one of the men was Ivan Ferrier, or if these two were the other party involved in the upcoming meeting.

John pulled his cell phone out of his pocket, and using Karl's SIM card began typing a message to send to Ivan. He chose a simple message. *Are you there yet?* and mashed the Send button with his thumb.

A few seconds later, one of the two men, the leader, grabbed his phone from his inside coat pocket and looked at the screen. He thumbed the screen for a moment, then dropped his hands while continuing to hold the phone.

Seconds later, John's phone buzzed with a text alert. He looked at the screen.

Yeah. Why?

The man with the fancy suit was Ivan. John didn't bother to send a reply. He just sat in the car until the two men walked into the warehouse. Then he slipped out of the car, closed the door gently, and made his way to the target building. He checked his watch and saw that it was ten minutes away from the scheduled time of the meeting.

His plan was to get in and grab Ivan before the meeting started. The fewer threats he had to deal with, the better. Neutralizing the second man would be key, to make sure no one would send an alert for as long as possible.

John moved to a side door halfway down the length of the building. He knelt in front of the handle and pulled the lockpicks from his pocket survival pack. A few seconds later, he turned the tumbler, pressed the thumb lever over the handle, and eased the door open.

Someone turned on all the lights just before John got in. The inside of the warehouse was brighter than outside, and the overhead lights got brighter as they warmed up. It seemed as if Ivan wanted no surprises during his meeting.

The inside of the building was a large, open area, with a concrete floor and a high ceiling that had visible steel support beams. The warehouse was less than halfway full, with boxes loaded on pallets, stacked mostly around the perimeter. The center of the large room was mostly bare, with only a table and six folding chairs adorning the empty area.

There were only a few dark spaces where John could hide, so he would have to execute his plan quickly. Luckily, his extensive military training and experience included objectives like securing a target. However, John usually worked as part of a team. He would have to adapt and do it solo. That was also what he had been trained to do.

* * *

Five minutes before the scheduled meeting time, another sedan, this one black, rolled into the designated warehouse lot, parking at the far end. The engine idled for a few moments before it was turned off. Each of the four doors of the car opened, and the four occupants got out. The driver and one of the rear passengers were both dressed in black suits with white shirts and black ties. They were heavily muscled, and their heads were on swivels, scanning the area for potential danger.

The front passenger was also in a suit, but it seemed a much more expensive cut and material. He wore a large jeweled gold watch, a couple of large rings, and a gold necklace, under his jacket but over his tie. He also glanced around, but more as a reflex to find people who might be admiring his look and style.

The last man exited the vehicle clutching a laptop case under one arm like it was a schoolbook. He was dressed in a short-sleeved light blue button-up shirt and khaki pants with brown shoes. Like the first three, he surveyed the area. Unlike them, his movements were quick and nervous, as if he were about to get caught doing something he wasn't supposed to be doing.

When the two muscled men were satisfied that the area was clear, they flanked the other two men and made their way toward the warehouse entrance. The flashier man walked one step in front with a cocky stride, with the nervous man shuffling right behind him.

* * *

John stalked the two men who were already inside as they checked the warehouse interior, using any shadows or objects large enough to conceal his considerable bulk. He moved like a ghost as he closed the distance to Ivan and his associate. A quick glance at his watch showed he had just under five minutes to grab his mark and get him out of the warehouse before the other people showed up. The time to act was now.

He moved to a position just beside the two men and lunged out from between two crates, hurling a massive fist right at Ivan's jaw. It was a blow that would have dropped just about any other man, but Ivan, by sheer luck or skill, saw the punch a split second before it landed. He turned his head away at the moment of impact, avoiding the most brutal part of it but still taking a considerable shot just above his ear. He was dazed and barely able to stay on his feet.

John used the opening to turn his attention to the second man. He pulled the stunned man closer, slipping behind him with surprising agility. John wrapped his left arm around the neck of the man, trying to secure a chokehold.

Before John could knock the second man out, Ivan regained his composure and whirled on the two combatants. He slid a hand into his suit jacket, pulling out a Kahr Arms PM9 pistol. John used his free right hand to clear his Colt 1911 from its holster inside his waistband while holding the man in front, using him as a barrier. John flicked the safety off, and had his weapon up and pointed at his hostage before Ivan could bring his gun up.

"Drop it," John said.

Ivan ignored the command. He whipped his pistol up and started shooting his PM9 wildly at them. The first shot went wide to John's left, but the follow-up shots impacted his human shield. The man bucked and screamed. John shoved him toward Ferrier, allowing him to roll behind a wooden crate.

John had overestimated the value of Ivan's partner. Bullets were crashing into his cover, and he could hear Ivan yelling now.

"You rats trying to ambush us!" he screamed as he reloaded.

John used the crates as cover, moving around to flank his target, preferring to let him shoot at his last known location. Ivan quickly sidestepped a crate to get a clear shot, only to find an empty space.

John stepped out from behind his cover, lining up his shot. His gun boomed twice, and two impacts hit Ivan's chest like sledgehammers, taking the gunman off his feet. John's shots had found their mark, as they had many thousands of times before during constant drilling and real-world execution. Ivan lay sprawled out on the floor, nearly unconscious.

John kept his Colt aimed at the downed man, closing the distance with smooth, deliberate steps, and kicked the PM9 across the floor. A quick glance confirmed his gut instinct. Ivan was wearing body armor under his suit. It was a clear sign that he didn't trust the people with whom he had been about to meet. Now John only had to secure him and get clear of the warehouse before the others arrived.

***

Parker Lewis fidgeted behind his boss, Dimitri. The two men assigned to guard them stood to either side and began to escort them to the warehouse for the scheduled meeting. He just wished he could back out of this whole thing.

He had been introduced to Dimitri a few weeks ago while at a company party. Dimitri was, for whatever reason, very interested in hearing about the type of work he did. Parker Lewis was a programmer and software security analyst for a major telecommunications company.

He and Dimitri had seemed to hit it off right away, and Parker was invited to party with the crazy Ukrainian two days later. He spent days treated like a VIP, getting into any place he wanted, while being told how important his work was.

At first, he'd suspected that this was just an attempt to recruit him to a different company. That would have been fine, but Parker didn't know how they would react if they offered him a job and he declined. He was happy with and well compensated by his current employer and wasn't looking to go anywhere else.

He hadn't realized at the time that he was being manipulated and recruited for a different purpose. All the talk of his importance eventually led to Dimitri offering Parker a one-time consulting job.

The job would pay nearly half his annual salary for only a few days' work. Also, they would pay him in cash, so there would be no evidence of any conflict of interest with his current employer. It sounded too good to be true, and part of him was reluctant to accept the offer.

When Parker voiced his concern about taking on the job, Dimitri's demeanor changed. His smile never faltered, and his temper never rose, but he fixed his eyes on Parker, and his words made it very clear that Dimitri was not a man to be refused. He mentioned Parker's mother and little brother, and how it would be unfortunate for them if he turned the offer down. The conversational tone of Dimitri's voice hid none of the threat that soaked every word he uttered.

So now here Parker was, flanked by two very muscular men, being led to a secret meeting late at night by this dangerous, unpredictable man. They were no more than 20 feet from the car when pops of gunfire came from inside the warehouse. The two security men pushed Parker down to a crouch and moved themselves to the front of the group.

"We're getting you out of here, sir," one of the guards said to Dimitri.

"No way! We're not leaving without what I came here for," was his reply to the guards.

Dimitri reached into his pocket and pulled out a small round object, slightly larger than a Zippo lighter. He held the disk against one of his nostrils and took in a sharp snort, wincing for a moment and shaking his head, as if to clear it. He looked more energized now.

"One of you stay out here with the geek." Dimitri gestured to Parker. "We'll see what's going on in there."

The two guards exchanged looks of uncertainty but decided to obey his commands. One of the guards ushered Parker back into the car. Dimitri unholstered a gold-plated MAC-10 submachine gun.

He and the other guard stayed partially crouched while moving at a brisk pace toward the front entrance of the warehouse. The main door was clear glass and led into a front area that resembled an office waiting room. The lights were on, but the room was empty.

Dimitri and his guard continued through an entryway at the end of the office and down a hallway with three doors. The first door led to a small bathroom; the second door, on the opposite wall, was just a small office for one person. The third door, at the end of the hall, was on the same wall as the little office and was the entry door to the main warehouse storage. Dimitri nodded to the guard, who brought his gun up.

* * *

John used his Spyderco Paramilitary tactical folding knife to cut sections of hard plastic bands that were used to secure shipping boxes onto pallets. He used them to restrain Ivan's wrists behind his back. John was beginning to bind his ankles when the sound of the door leading into the warehouse caught his attention, followed by a man yelling.

"What the hell is this?" a man in an expensive-looking suit holding an expensive-looking gun, shouted.

It seemed the other party had arrived a little early to the meeting as well. It seemed neither side trusted the other. John knew he couldn't just explain his way out of this situation. His best bet would be to create enough of a distraction to get his target out of the building.

The larger of the two men moved up to take the lead, holding his pistol with both hands. The gaudy-looking man followed close behind, holding his shiny

SMG in one outstretched hand. The man spotted John and started spraying lead while cackling like a maniac.

John slid along the ground behind a stack of crates. He could hear the stuttering barks from the MAC-10 and the peppering pops from the other man's handgun. Splinters flew as bullets pounded into the wood, forcing John to stay behind his cover.

Looking for an opportunity to strike, he heard the crazy man shouting orders to his bodyguard while reloading his weapon. John dove and rolled behind a pair of steel barrels and came up just high enough to aim over his new cover, firing his 1911 at the two attackers.

The man in the shiny shirt and jewelry leaped to the side, spraying bullets in return. The bigger bodyguard wasn't so lucky. Three .45 caliber slugs punched into his torso and exploded from the man's back.

Ivan regained consciousness and struggled to his feet. He saw the firefight occurring nearby and made a break for the nearest exit. The crazy man with the gold submachine gun fired a burst at the fleeing man, sending chips of concrete and sparks from metal support beams raining down.

John fired several rounds, forcing the shooter to drop back down. He slapped a fresh magazine into his 1911 as his opponent fired back at him. The two combatants found themselves in a stalemate. *Gotta get him to pop out,* John thought as he peeked between the barrels.

His attacker crouched behind several pallets of mechanical parts, with a steel support beam a few feet back to one side. John's eye caught the base of a red steel cylinder. A fire extinguisher. John acted fast, sliding out to his left, giving himself a clear shot. The pistol bucked in his hand as his round punched a neat little hole in the bottom corner of the fire extinguisher, sending out a cold stream of CO_2 behind the pallets.

He shifted his front sight as the man behind cover leaped up, startled by the sudden pop and hiss behind him. John double-tapped his target, causing two red blooms to appear on the man's chest and sending him staggering back into the growing cloud.

Getting back to his feet, John kept his weapon trained on the crazy man's position as he headed over to Ivan's prone body. A pool of blood was spreading out from under his body up along the left side of his jacket. John turned the man over, glancing down at the bullet wound under his arm where his body armor didn't cover him sufficiently.

John pressed a hand to the wound to slow the bleeding. He used his other hand to shake Ivan's head and face, trying to get the wounded man to respond.

"Ivan. Ivan, who's your boss?" John asked. "I can call him to get you help if you tell me who he is, or how I can reach him."

He shook the man's head a few more times. Ivan's eyes swam side to side. His breathing slowed until it finally stopped. John patted the pockets of Ivan's suit, pulling out a wallet, a set of car keys, and a flash drive stashed in the inner jacket pocket. He held the small storage device up, running a thumb across the anodized aluminum sleeve. He put the drive into his pocket and looked for any relevant contact information inside the wallet.

Finding only cash and credit cards, he tossed it back onto Ivan's chest and stood up. John walked over to the other two bodies, finding nothing of interest. He would have to get the drive to Jennifer to see what was on it.

* * *

"Stay here," the guard said to Parker after the firefight had stopped.

The big man retrieved his pistol and pulled the slide back slightly. Satisfied that his weapon had a round in the chamber, he jogged toward the front entrance.

The door opened and a large figure stepped out, backlit by the interior halogen lights. The bodyguard was using a hand to shield some of the light when the man raised a weapon and shot him three times in the sternum.

Parker panicked, scrambling around in the seat, trying to decide if he should climb into the driver's seat or hide. By the time Parker looked back up, the stranger had already covered the distance to the car, like a slasher movie serial killer. He pulled the driver's side door open and pointed a pistol at Parker.

"You're not going to give me any trouble, are you?" the man asked in a gruff, no-nonsense voice.

"I don't want any trouble. I didn't even want to come here tonight."

"I'll take that as a *no*. Just sit back and don't try anything, or I'll give you a couple of extra breathing holes."

Parker sat back, clutching his laptop case to his chest.

The man started the car using the keys retrieved from the dead guard and drove away from the immediate area. He pulled the car over to the side of the road five minutes later and killed the engine. The imposing man turned to face Parker.

"What's your name?"

"P-P-Parker. Lewis. Parker Lewis." he stammered.

"Alright, Parker, what was it you were sent here to do?"

"I don't know," he said. "Honest. I heard something about verifying some kind of code-breaking algorithm. Like, CIA stuff."

The man stared at him for several tense moments.

"My name is John," the man finally said. "I'm going to take a wild guess and say you weren't real close with those guys back there."

"Like I said, I didn't even want to be here."

"You're going to help me out, Parker," John said. "And if you do what I ask, I'll let you go."

Parker didn't have the honed senses to tell if someone was lying to him, but any chance at staying alive worth taking. "W-whatever you need."

John held up a slim aluminum stick with a USB connector on the end. "First, what's on this?"

Parker paused for a second before nodding and reaching out for the flash drive. He opened his laptop and inserted the device into his computer. The drive contained only a single directory, with three separate directories inside. He spent a few seconds browsing the contents of each.

"These are collections of personal information on three different people."

"Who are they?" John asked.

"I, uh, I can't find that info," Parker said. "At least not yet."

"Okay. You've got about forty-five minutes," John said,   starting   the   car   again.

CHAPTER

12

DAY 2   06:31 Mountain Time

Warren Ratcliffe sat at the table on his balcony, sipping his black coffee and looking at the mountain view as the sun rose. He kept to his rituals, always waking early enough to eat his breakfast while the sun rose. It was one of the many traits that made him a successful man. While the rest of the world lay in their beds, drooling and snoring, he was already putting his power and resources to work, building an empire.

A quiet, unassuming older man set a tray down in front of Warren with his breakfast of poached eggs and freshly smoked slab bacon. Mr. Gordon's soft footfalls contrasted the servant's shuffling steps. He walked onto the balcony as the other man left, settling next to the table, far enough away to allow Warren to enjoy his breakfast, but close enough to let him know that he had somewhat important news.

Warren finished a bite and wiped the cloth napkin down over his mouth as he swallowed. "What is it, Mr. Gordon? What's so urgent that I can't sit here and enjoy my breakfast in peace?"

Not the type to back away from the aggressive tone Warren used, Gordon took a step forward.

"There has been no contact with Mr. Ferrier since the meeting three hours ago."

Even through the mirrored sunglasses he wore, Warren could see the man's piercing gaze, like the reflection of the sunrise in the lenses were intense beams shooting from Gordon's eyes.

"What about Karl?" Warren asked.

"Karl has been out of reach since last night," the enforcer said. "I have men heading out to the last known location. I will let you know what they find out."

Warren threw the napkin down and slapped both of his palms on the table, rattling the plates and silverware. He could feel the blood rushing through his ears, and his vision reddened.

"It's a double cross. Some greedy little worm sold us out."

He grabbed the napkin and wiped away the hot coffee that had splashed onto his hand as he looked up at his right-hand man.

"Get back out there and find out what happened."

Mr. Gordon answered with a nod, turned on his heels, and strode back into the mansion.

* * *

Emily lay on her side with her knees pulled close to her body. Her mind raced through various escape plans, but all of them ended badly for her. She was unable to maintain focus, her mind returning too often to the murder of her father. She prayed that her mother was okay.

Her body involuntarily stiffened when she heard the soft click and slide of the lock on the door. A man walked in holding a tray with a plate and cup. He put the tray on the floor, close to her bed.

Like many of the others in the house, he wore a dark military-style uniform and kept his sandy blonde hair cropped close to his scalp. His ears stuck out a bit more than normal, and his tanned skin lessened the contrast between his light hair and hazel eyes.

"Just leave the tray by the door when you're finished. I'll be back a little later to pick it up."

Watching the man closely, Emily replied with a short nod.

The door latched closed behind him, and the lock slid back into place. She knelt next to the tray, examining it all like a bomb disposal officer. On the plate was a vegetable omelet and some wheat toast. There was a cup of water, but there were no utensils. The tray and cup were plastic, but the plate felt like it might be ceramic. Emily processed the new information, making adjustments to her plan of escape.

She scooped up a chunk of the omelet with her hand and stuffed it into her mouth. She took a bite of the toast as well. Emily wasn't sure if it was the quality of the food or the comfort it brought her after the long hours of stress, and sadness, but she found herself devouring her meal. She gulped the spring water to wash it all down, and wiped her mouth with the sleeve of her uninjured arm, setting the paper napkin supplied with the meal to the side for later use.

She brushed the remaining crumbs from the plate and brought it up to examine it closer. Her plan now was to break the plate and hide a shard away with her new lockpicks. She would have to wrap it in the napkin to help keep it hidden.

CHAPTER
13

DAY 2   07:53 Mountain Time

"No Easy Way Out"
Robert Tepper

Jennifer pulled her metallic gray Lexus NX into her assigned company parking spot. She left the engine running as her hands tightened on the steering wheel. Her eyes darted up to the rearview mirror, looking for the security detail. There was no sign of them nearby, although she could see them following as she left the house earlier.

I guess no sign of them is a good thing, she thought. She turned the engine off and stepped out of her car, smoothing the navy blue jacket of her pantsuit before buttoning it up. She straightened and tugged the collar of her cream-colored dress shirt, more out of ritual than any need to adjust her attire. Staring at her reflection in the tinted window, Jennifer inhaled deeply and let the breath out through her mouth in one smooth drawn-out exhalation, letting the relaxation settle in.

She pulled her purse tight to her body, walking toward the front entrance as her fingers found the edge of the plastic ID badge clipped to her lapel. She pulled it free and stepped toward the sensor to scan the chip inside her badge to gain access to the building. Her hand shook as her arm extended. Her heart raced, and a sense of dread draped across her shoulders like a thick blanket. She struggled to breathe, thinking about Emily and what the kidnappers were asking of her.

"Can I get that for you?"

The sudden voice snapped Jennifer out of her panicked state. She pressed her lips together and put on a wistful smile, turning to face the young man approaching.

"Uh, yeah, thanks. I think I'm having a bit of trouble with my badge," Jennifer said.

He smiled and scanned his own, unlocking the door. "You first, Ms. Dawson." He gestured inside while holding the door open.

"Thank you." She gave him a nod and turned away to head inside before he could see the fear pull her features back down.

Her heels clicked to match her rapid steps, as she headed straight to her office, wasting no time. Her mind walked through the various steps to take possession of the device. Just a straightforward sign in using her security credentials would get her into the research-and-development wing. From there, she needed to head to the secure data division where they were working on the PEST prototype.

As one of the key members of the team, Jennifer knew that getting the device into her hands wasn't going to be difficult. Gaining possession of it and swapping it for the replica were the easy parts. From there she knew that removing the prototype from the secure area would be the tricky step. Just walking in, heading straight to the device, and walking back out would raise too many suspicions.

At her desk, Jennifer pulled out a mostly empty notebook, scribbling some phony formulas and parameters onto one of the pages. She would pretend to run some diagnostics, using the decoy notes to make it look like she would be confirming some of the numbers, and then put the fake where the team kept the original.

For anyone involved in the project, the process was straightforward and by the book, which was why the kidnappers had targeted Emily. The perfect leverage. Once they got their hands on the PEST device, they wouldn't care what happened to Jennifer, so the paper trail of possession didn't matter to them.

Her biggest concern would be Emily's safety once the authorities were alerted to the missing prototype. They would look at her as the primary suspect. She would need to tell them the truth and hope to avoid arrest. There was no doubt in her mind that IntelliSys would discover the theft of the device within hours. Possibly even minutes. The only thing that mattered to her now was getting her daughter back.

* * *

Emily stood away from the bed, holding the plate up at chest height with an outstretched arm. In her other hand, she held on to the plastic tray with the cup resting on it. Her breathing quickened as she tried to scoot her feet away, fearing the sharp chunks from the plate once it hit the stone floor. Emily bit her lip and released the plate and tray at the same time, stepping away as quick as she could.

The plate hit almost flat, but one end struck just before the other end, and the plate smashed into many pieces. The industrial plastic tray and cup clattered among the ceramic debris. It was loud enough to create a convincing cover story. Emily crouched next to the mess and scanned the pieces, looking for something usable. Something that could function as a tool or a weapon.

She sifted through with extended fingers before finding a long, sharp piece that fit her needs. She heard heavy footsteps approaching and snatched the chunk quickly, wrapping it up in the paper napkin, careful not to slice her hand open. She tucked the wrapped shard into her cast, wedging it into a small space along the inside of her forearm. She winced in pain from both the ache of her injury and the sharp edge pressing into her soft skin.

She staggered back several steps with a look of guilt on her face. She couldn't contain her natural reaction, but it ended up working for her as the man barged in and looked down at the mess on the floor.

"It was an accident. I was trying to bring it to the door." The fear and stress caused her eyes to well up and redden, helping to sell it even more. "I just wanted to help."

The guard wasted no time grabbing the tray and gathering the largest of the pieces to pile up onto it. He kept asking to make sure Emily was okay and glancing back over his shoulder to the still-open door.

Is he afraid? Will they kill him too if something happens to me? Emily took a step forward, almost feeling sorry and wanting to help, but the guard put up a hand and gestured for her to stay back.

She went back to the bed and sat with one leg tucked underneath, finally able to relax. She kept her posture and demeanor casual, scanning the room, not trying to look like she was watching the man clean up her mess. Emily was glancing out into the hall when another man stormed in, upset at what he saw.

He walked over to the mess, berating the other man, but he kept glancing over at Emily and looking away. The two men exchanged quiet words, and Emily couldn't hear what they said. The first man's tone was softer, more apologetic. His position was lower than that of the second man, both physically and in rank. The second man stole a glance at Emily before turning to the door and closing it behind him just enough to cut off her line of sight outside the room. The first guard gathered the rest of the larger chunks, leaving bits of sharp ceramic and a fine layer of dust.

"I'll be back with a broom to get the rest of this." He pointed to the mess with a toe, not even looking at Emily.

As he reached the entrance, the door opened again and the second man grabbed the tray while shoving a broom and dustpan into the first man's chest. The exchange was awkward, and again they spoke in sharp, quiet sentences. The guard turned, keeping his head down, and swept up the mess. Emily held her arms folded across her stomach and did her best to maintain her casual front.

The man finished the chore and nodded to her as he left, never taking his eyes off the ground. The door latched shut, and after a few long seconds, the lock slid and clicked into place. She released a slow, shaky breath and pulled the bundled napkin from her cast. Her hands trembled as she unwrapped the shard and examined it.

The piece of the plate tapered out to 3 inches in length, ending in a sharp point. The edge along one side felt razor sharp as Emily ran a thumb down from the point. She kept glancing up at the door, expecting someone to barge in at any second.

She wasn't sure how the shard of ceramic would be of any use, but it was important to gather as many useful tools and possible weapons as she could. A lesson she had learned from her father about always being prepared. It also gave her piece of mind knowing it was available.

Laying the napkin out, Emily retrieved the makeshift lockpicks she had made from the toilet paper roll spring and placed them with the piece of broken plate, then wrapped everything up as small as she could before sliding the bundle back into her cast.

* * *

Jennifer put her hand on the latch of her office door and closed her eyes. She kept reminding herself that she was doing this for Emily. She took two quick breaths through her nose and exhaled through her mouth before stepping out into the hall.

Her shoes clicked in a steady rhythm as she strode to the R&D department. She held her badge in her left hand, ready to swipe the RF chip at the card reader to gain access. As she turned the corner and covered the last 20 feet, Jennifer saw a guard posted in front of the entryway. Her heart raced, but this was standard procedure.

"Morning," she said, doing her best to keep her emotions in check.

"Good morning, Ms. Dawson."

She scanned her badge, keeping her smile as bright as she could without straying into overly excited. The electronic lock clicked, and she pulled the door open, heading inside and giving the guard a quick nod as she passed. Gritting her teeth, Jennifer took another few short breaths, stuffing her hands in her pockets to hide the shaking.

The area reserved for the PEST project had no additional security posted, but removing the hardware itself from the locked containment required clearance credentials. That was the easy part. Right now, her biggest issue was the people currently working on the project. After hours would be the best time, but Jennifer didn't have that luxury. She was being forced to pull this off during regular business hours.

The project supervisor, Simmons, finished talking to an intern, sending the young man on an errand as Jennifer walked up.

"Morning, Jen." He gave only a quick glance up before looking down at some figures and sipping his coffee.

"Hey, Simmons."

She stood in place far too long for anyone else in her situation.

"Can I help you with anything?" he asked, looking back up.

"I, uh, the prototype has been spitting out some strange packets in a couple of the test runs," Jennifer said, doing her best to come up with something on the spot.

"Oh?" He shuffled a few sheets around on his desk. "You mean, like, artifacts or garbage data?"

"I'm not sure. I just need to hook it up to a workstation and run a few tests."

"No need. I can have my team take care of that. Just give me the parameters you're using, and we'll just—"

"No, no. You don't need to waste their time." Her heart hammered. "I don't want to mess with their schedule."

He gave her a quizzical look. "Are you sure? I mean, it's no trouble. They're ahead of schedule right now."

"Yeah. It's just a quick test," Jennifer said. "It would probably take longer to write down the test-cycle parameters anyway."

Simmons stared at her, trying to figure out the puzzle before him. His expression softened.

"I suppose you're right," he said. "It's not every day we get ahead of schedule, and we'll need all the padding we can get when the guys upstairs start dumping the feature creep on us, right?"

They both laughed. It was a genuine emotion, one that Jennifer hadn't felt since before the call from the kidnappers.

"Thank you, Simmons."

They walked over to the *vault* where the device prototype sat. Jennifer was stepping forward to swipe her badge when Simmons held up a hand.

"I got it." He slid his badge across the matte dark gray plastic covering the scanner, and the door slid open. "Just, you know…just let me know if you find any odd data output we should be concerned with."

"I will. Thanks."

Jennifer walked into the vault, balling up her hands tightly to keep the shaking down. Coming up with convincing lies was not one of her marketable skills, and nothing she said should have convinced Simmons to let her in. The only reason he didn't call security had to be because there was no reason in the world to suspect her of attempted corporate espionage and theft.

She brushed two fingers across her forehead to swipe a stray lock of hair, feeling a light layer of sweat. The room's climate control kept the temperature low, but her nerves counteracted that.

Jennifer pushed the glass case back on its hinges, exposing the PEST device. She ran the pad of her thumb along the machined aluminum edges of the black anodized case. She pulled out the decoy, an early-concept version inside a similar shell, that she'd had at home.

Before she could talk herself out of moving ahead with the plan, Jennifer dropped the original into her purse. To keep up appearances, she carried the fake over to one of the workstations and pretended to run a quick series of tests, making sure the displays faced away from any prying eyes.

She knew her nervous glances would attract attention if she hung around too long, so the "test runs" took less than a minute before she packed everything up. Once they noticed the device inside was a fake, security officers would swarm the building. Jennifer just needed enough time to get back to her car.

As the glass case clicked back into place, sealing the decoy prototype in, Jennifer realized that the logs would show Simmons giving her access to the room. He would be the primary suspect until he implicated her, or they reviewed the security camera footage. It could give her the window she needed to get the prototype out.

An eerie calm washed over her as she focused only on the task at hand. *I've got to bring the device to the men that have Emily, and get her back.*

CHAPTER

14

"I'm That Type of Guy"
LL Cool J

Mr. Gordon adjusted the cuff of his shirt. He was dressed in a security uniform, using the disguise to infiltrate IntelliSys and get to the monitoring station. The guard on duty lay slumped in his chair with his head lolling to one side, neck broken.

The bank of monitors along the wall of the small office showed the feed from all the cameras, in a matrix. The footage from every camera was linked to the same bank of drives to store the video digitally, but monitors displayed them all in a grid of smaller windows.

The enforcer called up the feed from an individual camera to fill one of the monitors. He leaned forward, putting his hands on the desk to get closer to the video of Jennifer talking her way into the room with the PEST prototype.

Jennifer made it into the room and swapped out the device with a decoy. She stashed the actual device, and brought the faux prototype to a nearby workstation and pretended to run some tests with it.

"She may have a future in espionage," Mr. Gordon said to the dead man seated next to him.

He watched the video long enough to confirm that she kept the device on her, putting the fake back into the vault. Mr. Gordon pulled a tablet device from the pouch that kept it strapped to his right thigh. He sent a message, reporting the current situation, and slipped it back into its *holster*.

Moving on to the next stage of his plan, he knelt next to a large duffel bag and pulled out several small packs. Each was an explosive device that would ensure the destruction of the data on the drives storing the security feed.

He grabbed a large metallic cylinder and twisted one of the ends 180 degrees, activating a series of lights showing that the explosive canister was in full communication with the trigger device and the other smaller devices on the hard drives.

Satisfied with the setup, Mr. Gordon pulled the brim of his hat down close to his brow and shouldered the bag, walking out. He locked the door behind him, secure in the knowledge that no one would be able to watch him as he moved through the building.

He spent the next few minutes walking the inner perimeter of the building, heading to key structural points and exits, placing more of the cylindrical explosive devices. These were slimmer canisters containing incendiary chemicals, with magnets to secure them to anchor points out of sight from casual observers.

* * *

Two men sat in a gray sedan parked at the far end of the IntelliSys parking lot watching the entrance. Both had their seatbelts off, preparing for a long wait for their quarry to come back out. The older of the two was brushing a hand over his beard when the second man tapped his shoulder.

"There she is," the younger man, Finn, said.

The bearded man, Officer Wells, checked his watch, noting that Jennifer walked out of the building through the main entrance less than two hours after she had gone in. She walked straight to her car, leaving for the day. Her stride was too long, and her steps were too quick. She glanced over her shoulder more than once.

"She's leaving already?" Finn asked.

They saw the brake lights of her car come on as the car started. She backed out of her parking spot and pulled out, heading for the main exit. The older man started the car, pulling his seatbelt over his shoulder, preparing to follow.

A faint buzz came from Finn's inside coat pocket, and he pulled his phone out. His eyes scanned the message, but he stared at it for a few more seconds to absorb it. He pulled up his contact list, scrolled down to near the bottom, and tapped the contact number with no listed name.

Their car pulled into traffic just as Jennifer made a left turn. The voice on the other end of the phone answered the younger officer's call.

"She's leaving right now," he said. "We're following now. She won't see us."

He listened to the call, then answered, "Yes, sir. We received the message from your man, Gordon. He confirmed she does have the device."

He pointed frantically before putting a hand over the mic on his phone. "Make this next right. We can cut her off at the next block," he said.

"Do you want to drive?" Wells asked, flipping up the turn signal to take the other man's suggestion.

He listened as the voice continued giving him detailed instructions. The only indication that he was still on the phone was an occasional grunt of assessment every few seconds. Finn ended the call and slipped the phone back into his pocket.

"What did they say?"

Finn looked over at his partner. "We follow her home."

"What if she doesn't go home?" The driver kept his eyes fixed ahead.

"Well then, you get to put your driving skills to the test and force her somewhere without any prying eyes so we can get our hands on that device."

"And what about her?"

The young man pulled his pistol from its shoulder rig and pinched the front of the slide, easing it back just enough to ensure that there was a round in the chamber. "We tie up all loose ends."

* * *

Mr. Gordon finished securing the last of the incendiary devices. He glanced down the hallway in both directions, smiling at the unsuspecting employees walking throughout the building. His cover remained intact.

He tossed the now empty duffel bag into a storage closet on his way to the nearest exit. As the heavy steel door of the back exit closed behind Gordon, he tapped out a series of digits on his tablet, triggering the security locks throughout the building. He heard the whirring clack from the lock confirming that the code had worked, trapping everyone inside.

He put away the tablet and retrieved a slim black polymer box with a pressure switch running along one side. His thumb slid along the back edge, finding the recessed power switch and clicking it into its *on* position.

A small amber light flashed three times before changing to a steady green. He continued walking away as his fingers closed in on the lever, activating the remote detonator.

A deep rumble shook the earth, followed by a series of muffled booms. Gordon slipped the detonator back into his pocket and tossed his hat like a Frisbee with the other hand as the internal pressure wave shattered every outside window within milliseconds of one another.

Large billowing plumes of fire exploded out as Warren Ratcliffe's head enforcer maintained his same pace, his stride unbroken and expression unchanged.

CHAPTER

15

Day 2   09:42   Mountain Time

John sawed off another piece of steak from his plate and stuffed it into his mouth, following it with a chunk of eggs. He and Parker sat in a diner eating breakfast while they tried to find anything of use on Karl's SIM card.

The hacker nursed a piece of white toast and a cup coffee, heavy on the cream and sugar. Parker's fingers danced over the keyboard of his laptop. He was hoping to find anything that would lead John to the location of his goddaughter, Emily.

Parker kept the toast clasped between his teeth as he typed out several more strings of commands, initiating a subroutine to pull contacts that met certain criteria and cross checked them with recent calling patterns. He bit off a chunk of buttered bread and dropped it onto the small plate next to his coffee, wiping his hands together.

"That shouldn't take too long," he said to John. "There isn't much on the card, but the algorithms building a plausible call pattern eats up a lot of CPU."

"I have no idea what you just said, son."

Parker smiled. "It will *ding* when it's done."

"Right, got it. Like a TV dinner," John said.

"Uh, yeah. Just like that." Parker took another bite of toast, speaking again as he chewed. "So what's the deal with all of this?" He nodded toward the laptop.

John jabbed the last piece of steak on the plate with his fork. "A good friend of mine was murdered yesterday. His daughter, my goddaughter, was kidnapped."

Parker wanted to ask more questions to start connecting the dots, but he could see that John was still struggling with what had happened. He waited for the old soldier to continue in his own time.

"Emily's mother, Jennifer, works for IntelliSys, in their R&D department," John said. "It's pretty obvious that Emily is the leverage for the kidnappers to get their hands on whatever that company is developing."

"It does seem that way," Parker said.

"My contact at the CIA is helping out. He tasked the local police with assigning an undercover security detail for her," John said.

"So, what does the device do anyway?" Parker asked.

John inhaled and sat back. "I don't know, but from what I was able to piece together, it's a device that is supposed to be able to decrypt highly secure data at a fast rate."

The laptop dinged, and Parker pulled it closer and started scrolling through the results.

"I'm not sure about the rest of the details, but if they're brazen enough to kill for it, then it's got to be something pretty powerful," John said.

Parker nearly cut him off midsentence. "Hey, John, what did you say were the names of the officers providing security for Jennifer?"

"Uh, Wells and Finn," John said. "Why, are they in danger too?"

"No, not exactly." Parker paused to make sure what he saw was correct. "It may be nothing, but it looks like Karl received a call from Finn."

"When?" John sat upright in his seat.

"Uh, yesterday afternoon."

John's eyes widened. He bolted up and rushed for the door. "Stay put."

"I—what?" Parker whipped his head around to all of his gear, the plates on the table, and John getting into the car.

"You can't just leave me here! He just left me here."

CHAPTER
16

DAY 2   09:56 Mountain Time

"Shout at the Devil"
Mötley Crüe

Jennifer pulled her Lexus into the garage and turned off the engine. She gripped the steering wheel and tried to slow her breathing and calm down. Grabbing her purse, she clutched it close to her body as she walked into the house, closing the garage door.

The thermostat ran on a program that didn't account for her being home this early, so the room was colder than she expected. Jennifer placed her purse on the coffee table and walked to the hall to turn the heat up a couple of degrees.

She walked back into the living room and dropped onto the couch. The shaking in her hands died down as she rubbed them together to warm up. Leaning forward, she pulled the purse open to look at the device sitting inside. Jennifer held it close, examining the small metal case, studying all the little details she had never noticed during the day-to-day grind.

A knock on her front door startled her. No one would have known she was here unless they were watching her or the house. She tossed the PEST back into her purse and was standing up looking around when a second knock came on the door with more authority.

She kicked up one of the couch cushions, pushed the bag all the way to the back, and pressed it back down before heading to the door.

She thought about saying something to the person outside but decided to check who was at the door quietly. Looking through the peephole, Jennifer could see a tall bearded man. She recognized him as Wells, one of the officers assigned as surveillance. Letting out a slow exhalation, she relaxed and unlatched the deadbolt lock.

"Hey, is everything okay?" she asked, opening the door just enough to show part of her face.

"I hope so," the man said. "We just noticed you coming back home sooner than expected. Is there anything we can do to help?"

"Oh, uh, no I'm fine," Jennifer said. "I was just feeling a little under the weather. Figured I should just stay here and get some rest before I lose my mind."

"I understand." The man's facial expression relaxed. "If you don't mind, I'd like to come in and get a good idea of the layout of your home, so my partner and I can make sure we're covering key entry points."

Jennifer looked back in the house, toward the couch.

"It will give you peace of mind so that you can feel safe, Ms. Dawson."

"Yeah. I guess you're right." She took a step back and pulled the door open a little more.

Moving in with the door, Wells pushed it open hard, forcing Jennifer back so that she staggered on her heels. He covered the distance fast and grasped her wrist while Finn stood on the porch making sure no one outside could see what was happening before following them inside.

The younger officer, closed the door, locking it behind them. Jennifer struggled to break free, but Wells' size and aggression caught her off guard. He shoved her into the kitchen and forced her to sit at the dining table. Wells pulled his jacket open far enough to tuck it behind his holster as Finn followed them in.

Jennifer held her hands up, palms out. "What's going on? What do you want?"

The younger officer glanced at his watch as he stood next to his partner. "Let's not waste time here, lady. Where's the prototype?"

"What proto—"

Before she could finish, the bearded man hooked a hand under the end of the small dining table, hurling it across the kitchen as he stepped in close to her. She leaned back, flinching to get away.

"Search the place," he said to Finn.

"I don't know what you guys are talking about." Jennifer could hear wood splintering and glass smashing as the undercover officer tore the living room apart. "Please. I have no idea what you guys are looking for."

Wells wound up and whipped the back of his hand across her face, snapping her head to the side hard. He crouched down to get closer to her level and spoke slowly.

"Where is the prototype?"

"I got it," the younger man said, walking back into the kitchen, holding Jennifer's purse in one hand and the prototype device in the other. "She had it stuffed in the couch."

* * *

"Your guys are dirty, Mark," John said into the speakerphone as he pulled the car into a tight turn.

"What? I—" Mark said before he was cut off.

"One of them was in contact with the people that killed Frank," John growled.

"John, I'm sorry. I had no idea." Mark's voice, even through the low-quality speakers, had a genuine concern.

"If I find out you had anything to do with this…" John let his threat hang while he focused on driving.

"I promise you, I had nothing to do with this, John," Mark said. "I called in a few requests to local police sources. The sheriff's office assigned those men."

"So where is the leak, Mark?"

"The only thing I can think of would be local-level corruption," Mark said.

John stomped hard on the brakes, feeling a stuttering as the antilock brakes prevented his car from slamming into the cross traffic. He put the gas pedal down all the way, timing his crossing with a gap between the cars as he ran a red light.

Mark asked, "What do you need from me? I can get you some backup."

"We can't risk it," John said. "We don't know who can be trusted locally."

"John, you know I owe you and Frank my life. I would never do anything to hurt you guys. We're brothers in arms."

John weaved through the traffic as it grew thicker at the next intersection. "I'll call you back when I take care of this, Mark." He ended the call and made a hard left, running another red light.

* * *

Wells laughed. "The couch? You thought no one would find it there?" He looked over to his partner. "So what's your excuse? Why did it take you so long to find it?"

Finn flipped him off. "Just make the call. I'll keep an eye on her."

The older officer dialed his phone and waited for the call to connect.

"We've got the device," he said.

The call lasted for another minute as he made small sounds of agreement while nodding. He put the phone back into his pocket and walked over to his partner. Jennifer sat on the chair wiping away tears and a trickle of blood from the corner of her mouth.

"They're sending a guy to pick up the device," the big man said, holding the PEST prototype in his hand.

"What are we supposed to do after that?" Finn asked.

"They'll take it back to make sure it's legit. We wait for their call either way." He put the device into his outer coat pocket and checked his watch.

Finn took off his jacket, resting it on the back of one of the chairs in the kitchen. He readjusted his shoulder rig, making sure that Jennifer had no doubt that he was armed.

After several minutes there was a knock at the door. Wells opened the door and stepped back as a well-dressed man entered.

"Mr. Gordon," Finn said. "Wow, we didn't expect you to see this through personally."

The man glanced into the house, letting his eyes settle on Jennifer. "Something this important requires a higher level of responsibility."

Wells held the device, placing it in a handkerchief before gently wrapping it up. Gordon picked it up and nodded before putting it in his jacket pocket.

"Wait for my call. Don't let the woman leave until you hear back from me," he said to the corrupt officers.

* * *

"I'm going to take another look around," Wells said. "Make sure we didn't miss anything." He left the kitchen and headed to the hallway.

Jennifer felt the tears well up in her eyes again. Now that they had the device, there was no need for them to return Emily. She didn't care about her life, only that of her daughter now.

"She's just a child. Please let Emily go," Jennifer said.

Finn didn't say anything. He just maintained a steely gaze, rubbing his hands together.

"You don't need her anymore. I'll do whatever you guys want."

"Lady, I'm going to need you to shut your mouth. Don't make this harder than it has to be."

Wells let out a pained grunt from one of the back bedrooms. Finn turned his head, listening in case his partner needed help moving some heavy furniture. A crash came from the end of the hall.

"You need some help back there, Wells?"

"Please, I'm begging you," Jennifer said, on the verge of standing up from her chair.

The man pulled the pistol from his holster and pointed it at Jennifer's head. "I said shut up! Keep it up and I'll put a bullet in your head, then you won't have to worry about your daughter anymore."

Jennifer was crying now, struggling to maintain her composure. Emily's life was on the line. Finn pulled his hand back, ready to pistol-whip her into silence.

His hand abruptly stopped as it started its forward movement. An iron grip was locked around his wrist with machine-like pressure. The man was looking back, confused about what had happened when John Stone used his other hand to swat the handgun free.

John turned his body with the rotation of the disarming to wind up a back elbow strike that crushed the man's nose. As the corrupt officer exhaled, blood sprayed out, pouring from his face as he staggered back, falling on the upturned table and snapping one of the legs off.

The frightened man scrambled to his feet and took off for the front door. John grabbed the chair with the jacket hanging from the back and whipped it at him with a sidearm motion. The wooden furniture smashed into pieces, hurling his target forward, careening into the kitchen entrance.

John stalked the man as he scrambled on all fours to escape into the living room. The bloodied officer pulled himself to his feet using the couch and turned to face his attacker. He reached behind his belt with shaky hands and pulled a knife from a horizontal, scout-style sheath.

The man brought the blade across his body in a desperate swipe. John leaned his body back far enough to avoid the first slash and shuffled back a half step to stay clear of a second swing. Before Finn could try for a third attempt, John snapped a front kick into his stomach, doubling him over.

As the man bent forward, John brought his fist upward in a devastating uppercut that landed solidly. The impact sent the bloodied man sailing back over the couch. His body flew in an arc and came crashing down onto the coffee table. The back of his head shattered the glass top as his neck bent back on the metal frame with a crunch.

With one forceful shove, John thrust the couch to the side, clearing a path to the man lying on the floor whimpering in pain. His left arm shook and twitched. His right arm and both legs remained motionless.

John picked up a couch cushion from the floor and knelt next to Finn's prone form.

"Who do you work for?" John asked.

The man's reply came out garbled through the blood pouring from his mouth. The uppercut had knocked several of his teeth loose, and the crimson fluid was still flowing freely from his broken nose. He coughed and spat out some of the blood.

"I think I…broke my neck." His voice came out in strained pants.

"Answer my question," John said, leaning in close.

"Montana…police department."

John pressed the cushion to the Finn's face, pressing hard against the man's mouth and nose, making it difficult for him to breathe. He lifted the cushion after a few seconds.

"Give me a name, Finn."

The back-and-forth interrogation continued, with John pressing the cushion over Finn's face when he didn't cooperate. This man either had little information of value or it would take too much time and effort to get him to give up whatever he knew. He needed to find the man who had taken the device and get it back. It was the only leverage to get Emily back safely. There was no time for a drawn-out interrogation.

John pushed the cushion back over the man's face, drew his 1911, and pressed the muzzle against the fabric. He fired twice, two barely contained booms putting the man out of his misery.

He stood and tucked the handgun back into the holster inside his waistband, then headed back into the kitchen to check on Jennifer. He wiped a thumb across her face, wiping some of the blood away.

"Where's the other guy?" Jennifer asked, wide-eyed.

"He's taking a dirt nap in the spare bedroom," he said. "Are you okay? Did they hurt you?"

"I'm fine," she said, though her shaky voice wasn't convincing. "You need to get the prototype back. It's the only way to save Emily."

"I promise you I will get her back safely," John said. "Come on, I've got to get you somewhere safe, so I can focus on getting the device back."

John picked her purse up off the floor and handed it to Jennifer. He guided her to the front door before heading back into the living room. He pulled the dead man's body to one side and retrieved a set of keys from his pocket, tossing them aside. His hands rifled through the remaining pockets coming up empty.

"Are you looking for this?" Jennifer was crouched next to a jacket on the floor, near the remains of a chair. She held the officer's phone in her hand, showing it to John.

"Yeah. We'll take your car. Let's go."

CHAPTER

17

DAY 2   10:24 Mountain Time

Emily lay on the mattress, wiping away another tear. Rolling over to face the door, she heard a faint intermittent buzzing. Not knowing what it was, she got up and walked slowly to the door. As she was within reach of the knob, her sneaker squeaked on a tile and she paused, ready to run back to her bed.

The sound outside changed to a quick series of snorts before settling back to its normal rhythm. *He's snoring*, Emily realized. The guard posted outside her door had fallen asleep.

She pulled the tool stash from her cast, taking the makeshift lockpicks from the paper napkin. Emily pressed her ear to the door to make sure that what she heard was the man snoring. She sat on her knees and slid the folded wire into the lock, using it as a torsion wrench as she worked the rake across the pins.

She struggled for several minutes before switching to a different pick and making some adjustments to the folded wire. On her next attempt to pick the lock, working as quietly as possible, the latch slid open.

Emily slipped the lockpicks into her pocket and wrapped the napkin around the base of the shard of broken plate, holding it in her hand. She turned the knob slowly and opened the door just enough to peer out through the crack. After a few tense seconds, she pulled the door open a little more. Looking out into the empty hall, Emily stepped out. The sleeping guard was the only person nearby.

Leaving her shoes inside, Emily moved down the hallway wearing only her socks to keep the noise down. The room she had come from was at the end of the hall, and she saw two other doors along the same wall. At the end, the path turned to the right.

She reached the second door, just before the bend, but before she could check to see if it was locked, she heard footsteps coming from down the hall. Emily found herself in a desperate situation as her mind ran through all the options.

Hiding in a different room could work, but if the door was locked, she would be caught out in the open. She could fight, using the shard in her hand, but if the other guard woke up, they would outnumber her. Emily ran back to the room they had been keeping her in. She knew she could pick the lock, so this was the safest play.

The door settled shut just as the heavy boots rounded the corner. Emily hurried to retrieve the picks from her pocket and re-engage the lock. As the tumbler turned, the deadbolt clunked into position.

The snoring man made an odd half snort/half cough and grumbled as she heard his chair scraping on the tile floor. Emily held her breath, with the picks still in the keyhole. The pressure of her situation caused her to rush re-engaging the lock, making too much noise, which woke the guard up. She stepped back and grabbed the shard of the plate again.

"How is everything going?" the approaching man asked.

"Fine. Nothing out of the ordinary." The sleepy guard's voice had a hint of fatigue, but not enough for the other man to notice.

She could hear the faint voices out in the hall as she pulled the picks out and headed to the mattress, stashing the tools back in their hiding spot. Waking the guard had worked in her favor, as his pride wouldn't let him admit to the other guard that he had fallen asleep.

She would just have to wait for another opportunity and hope that the same guard would be posted later tonight. Emily sat back on the mattress, pulling her knees up to her chest and staring at her shoes next to the door. Now that she knew she could open the door with her salvaged lockpicks, her confidence rose.

I'm getting out of here tonight.

* * *

Warren walked over to the large window in his office, speaking through a Bluetooth headset. "Do you have the device, Mr. Gordon?"

"I've got it with me," Gordon said. "I met Wells and Finn at Ms. Dawson's house personally."

"Good. Bring the prototype back here, so we can authenticate it."

"I'm on my way now."

A smile crept across Warren's face. "Once we've ensured that the actual PEST device is in our possession, I need you to cover our tracks. Nothing is to lead back to me."

"Of course, sir. No loose ends."

Warren ended the call and dropped the Bluetooth earpiece and mic onto his desk. His smile grew. Even though there had been a couple of hiccups early on, he was starting to see the finish line. It was nearly time   to   celebrate.

137

CHAPTER
18

DAY 2   11:49 Mountain Time

"Burning Heart"
Survivor

John pulled Jennifer's Lexus up to the curb of the diner. He pulled his seatbelt off and opened the door, leaving the car running.

"Wait here," he said.

Jennifer nodded, finally able to catch her breath and relax. She turned to face the window, gasping as a frantic man came out of the diner moving quickly toward them. She was clutching the seatbelt, preparing for another gunfight, when she saw John wave him over.

"I can't believe you just left me like that, John," the man said, stowing his gear behind Jennifer. He climbed in and shifted to the center of the bench seat.

"There was no time, Parker. We're up against the clock now."

Parker Lewis leaned forward and presented a hand. "Hello, Mrs. Dawson. I'm Parker."

"Ms. Dawson," Jennifer said, reaching across her body to shake his hand. "Please, call me Jennifer."

He continued his tirade as John settled into his seat and started driving. "I don't have my wallet, John. You just pulled a *dine and dash*, sticking me with the bill for your steak and eggs. I almost had to wash dishes."

"A little honest work won't kill you," John said.

"How did you pay for the food?" Jennifer asked.

"Probably wasn't *honest work*," John said.

Parker let out a short mocking laugh. "I traded service for service. The manager now has all of the premium movie channels on his cable account, for free. That's far more valuable than any *food* they serve in there."

John shook his head, changing the subject. "Here," he said, handing a mobile phone to Parker. "We took it from one of the crooked cops."

Parker held it between his thumb and forefinger by one corner. "Is there any blood on it?"

"Relax, kid. It was in his jacket."

"Was his jacket full of holes?"

Jennifer turned to face him. "He didn't have it on when…" She let the statement drag out so Parker's mind could complete the scene.

Parker nodded, pulling the phone's SIM card out and dropping it into the small device plugged into his computer's USB port.

"We need to know what's next," John said. "If we don't start getting aggressive, the advantage will be lost."

"What are you going to do now?" Jennifer asked.

"We have to find out where the device is," John said. "From there, we can use it as leverage or, if we're lucky, it will lead us to the man at the top."

"What about my daughter?"

John stopped the car at a red light and looked over at Jennifer. "I will do everything in my power to get Emily back to you safely." He gripped the steering wheel and faced the front again. "And everyone that gets in my way will be put into the ground."

"I've got something," Parker said. "I cross-referenced the known numbers, and it looks like there are only three possible locations where we will be able to find who you're looking for."

"How close are they to each other?" John asked.

"Two are within five miles, but the third is pretty far away," Parker said, as his fingers danced across the keys.

"We don't have time to check three different locations that far apart. You're going to have to give me something better."

"Ask and ye shall receive," Parker said. "Check this out."

John pulled the Lexus into a parking lot as he and Jennifer turned to face the back seat. Parker held the laptop's display up, using his hand at an awkward angle to press the space bar.

"This was taken within the last twenty-four hours, from a traffic camera near possible location number three," the hacker said.

The footage showed a white van passing through the frame. There was visible damage on the side panel.

"What are we looking at?" Jennifer asked.

"Not much now. Just a van passing through. But…" Parker said, typing a few seconds more before spinning the screen back to face them.

"An hour before that video was taken, traffic cameras a couple of miles from Frank Colt's residence picked up the same van."

The second video showed a white van, with the same side-panel damage drive past.

"Where is that third location?" John asked.

Parker indicated the remote section on the map. "Door number three is the Ratcliffe estate. It's a nice big house out in the hills, about four or five hours west of Great Falls. Far enough from the rest of civilization to do some shady business."

"Who's Ratcliffe?" John asked.

"Warren Ratcliffe," Jennifer said. "He's connected with one of the smaller data management companies, but he's shown plenty of interest in our projects."

"Guy's a real corporate sleazeball," Parker added. "He's always caught up in some bad deal where people end up losing their shirts while he walks away clean."

John picked up his mobile phone and dialed a number.

"Who are you calling?" Parker asked.

"My friend, Mark," John said. "I'm going to need satellite pictures of the grounds so that I can plan my entry."

* * *

John parked the Lexus in his driveway, then led Jennifer and Parker into the house. He stayed outside for another moment to make sure no one had followed them.

In the house, Parker set his laptop up in the living room. He had the satellite images Mark had sent, showing the only major road leading to the remote house in the hills.

Jennifer sat on one end of the couch with her legs pulled up. She stared off into the distance, unable to focus on anything going on around her. The only thing she could think of was Emily.

"I put some coffee on," John said, stepping back into the living room.

"Hopefully it's not some cheap supermarket brand," Parker said. "I haven't had a decent cup since yesterday morning."

John gave Parker a look that told him everything he needed to know about the brand of coffee and what John thought of his opinion. The hacker looked back down at his laptop. "Yeah, anything's good, thanks."

"Stay inside," John said, looking more at Jennifer than Parker. "Don't make any outside contact with anyone other than me."

"Where are you going?" Jennifer asked.

"I'm going to get your daughter."

* * *

John closed the door to his bedroom and walked to the closet. Inside, he keyed in the four-digit code to open the large gun safe secured within. Playing out in his head the type of tactics needed, John changed into a long-sleeve black T-shirt and all-black BDU pants. He put on a pair of black Oakley military boots and hiked a ballistic vest over his torso, securing it tightly with the wide hook-and-loop straps on either side.

He reached into the safe and grabbed the battle belt, strapping it around his waist. He secured the Colt 1911 into the drop leg holster, and grabbed three more magazines and slid them into the pouches on his front-left hip.

Next was the H&K MP5 submachine gun with an integral sound suppressor. The nylon shoulder strap kept the weapon hanging under his left arm. The grip faced forward, so he could draw it across his body, keeping it out of the way but still ready to be deployed at a moment's notice.

Two spare mags found a home in the MOLLE webbing of his vest. On the left side of his belt, he attached the sheath containing a large KA-BAR Marine fighting knife.

Finally, John grabbed the M4 carbine and worked the charging handle to ensure that the weapon was clear. He brought it up to his shoulder to check the sights. John loaded the rifle and filled the pouches across his chest with spare magazines. Pulling the three-point tactical sling over his body, he let the weapon hang in the standard front carry position.

He pulled two radios from the top shelf of the safe before swinging the heavy steel door shut with his foot. John stepped back out into the living room to check on his guests, letting the comforting scent of brewing coffee relax him.

"What country did you say you were going to take over?" Parker asked. His eyes were fixed on John's gear, lingering on the military assault rifle strapped to his chest.

John handed Jennifer one of the radios. "You can use this to reach me. If anything happens here while I'm gone, I need you to let me know."

"Won't the bad guys hear the call?" Jennifer asked.

John strapped a LASH throat mic and inserted the earpiece into his right ear. "Not with this."

Scooping up the keys to Jennifer's car, he walked out of the house, locking the door behind him.

CHAPTER
19

DAY 2   16:16   Mountain Time

Mr. Gordon's shoes tapped out a rhythm with each step as he walked into the large office area of Warren's house. He pulled the PEST prototype from his coat pocket and placed it on the table.

Seated next to Warren was a mousey woman with wavy hair pulled into a loose bun. She reached forward to retrieve the device and hooked it up to her laptop. Her fingers tapped out a series of keystrokes, and she sat upright.

"This should only take a minute to verify," the mousey woman said.

"Good," he said in response.

Her eyes darted up and down as she read the data. "It's confirmed, sir. This is the device you're looking for."

"Thank you," Warren said. "Now please, if you'll excuse us."

The woman nodded, readjusted her glasses, and packed up her laptop. She left the room shuffling while leaning forward, like she was perpetually off balance. She veered her path to avoid Mr. Gordon, who came back into the room holding a box.

It was a special case designed to protect the prototype with shock-absorbing foam. The outer shell was a tough polymer reinforced with an embedded wire mesh. With the device settled into its custom-cut recess, Gordon shut the case and handed it back to Warren.

"Call your men and have them eliminate the Dawson woman," Warren said. "We can't risk anything coming back at us later."

Gordon nodded and pulled out his phone.

"And have someone kill the girl," Warren said, facing away.

"I'll see to it personally," he said. The enforcer would not enjoy killing a twelve-year-old girl, but he had no qualms about doing whatever it took to keep his client safe and free.

He left Warren in the room alone as he stepped out to send a text message to the men watching Jennifer Dawson.

* * *

Emily held her ear pressed to the hardwood door for minutes. She strained to hear any signs of the guard outside leaving or falling asleep. All she could hear was an occasional boot or chair readjusting. She retreated to her bed and sat with crossed legs, facing the door. Now was not the time to make her escape.

After what felt like hours, Emily's posture broke as she scooted farther back to lean on the wall. Her eyelids were starting to droop when another sound pulled her attention back. Boot steps approached, and she repositioned herself on the mattress to appear less conspicuous, just in case anyone opened the door.

A muffled conversation started on the other side. Emily scooted along the floor, trying to get close enough to hear what they were saying. Only a few feet from the door, she could hear a couple of words here and there.

"C'mon, man. She's just a little girl," the arriving man said. "Where's she gonna go?"

There was some trepidation in the voice of the posted guard as he replied. She held her breath, silently rooting for the other man to convince the guard to step away, mouthing the words *just go*.

Finally, the guard said, "Alright, you win. But I can't stay too long."

Emily let out her breath as the two sets of footsteps pounded away, receding in the distance. This opportunity would not be safe, and her mind argued for her to wait and make sure, but this might be the only chance she would get.

She scrambled the rest of the way to the door and pulled the lockpicks from her cast. With more confidence after having opened the door the first time, Emily was able to unlock the deadbolt in less than a minute. She put the lockpick into her back pocket and pulled out the ceramic shank wrapped in the napkin.

Again, she bundled the paper along the base to use as a handle and pulled the door open just a crack. Emily peered out into the now empty hallway, seeing the vacant chair up against the wall. No one was guarding her.

CHAPTER

20

"Raising Hell"
Run DMC

Leaving Jennifer's Lexus behind, John hiked the remaining mile to conceal his approach. The foliage along the hills afforded him the necessary cover to get close. He held the M4 carbine at a low ready position and moved with deliberate steps while keeping an eye out for guards or traps along the perimeter.

He covered the remaining quarter mile in ten minutes, approaching the compound from a secluded back area that he had marked out on the satellite images. The security presence looked high for a random rich man's house in the hills. That alone confirmed that this was the place.

Even with the increased manpower, he could see that the guards themselves were lax in their procedure. They had the guns and the bodies but lacked the discipline to maintain constant communication. They wouldn't be expecting some woman with a programming background to organize an assault on their home. Their hubris would bring about their downfall.

John was concealed behind some foliage as one guard walked the outside perimeter of the mansion's security walls and right past him. The guard stopped just 20 feet away from him to smoke a cigarette. Flicking open his lighter, he deftly lit the cigarette in his mouth, put the lighter back into his pocket, and inhaled. His face and posture radiated smug self-satisfaction at his practiced lighting technique.

Too bad he didn't spend his time practicing how to search for threats, John thought as he let the M4 hang on his off-side to bring the silenced MP5 across his body. There was a soft rustling of leaves that caught the smoking guard's attention. He turned as John brought the submachine gun to his shoulder. The guard didn't even fully grasp what was happening before the bullets struck him. The silenced MP5 chuffed three times, putting clean holes through the man's sternum.

John covered the distance fast, reaching the man's body just as it hit the ground. He grabbed a handful of the guard's pant leg, keeping his weapon shouldered with his right hand, and dragged the body into the bushes. He took the radio from the dead man and clipped it to his vest before he continued.

Another strip of trees and bushes led John to a clearing with several parked vehicles. An assortment of jeeps, trucks, commercial Hummers and motorcycles filled the provisional parking lot. He approached the loitering guard, still holding the MP5 in his right hand, this time pointed down.

Keeping his center of gravity low, John walked up in a partial crouch, reaching out with his left hand, preparing to wrap it around the man's mouth before bringing his right hand up to complete a quiet neck break.

Before he could execute his plan, a second guard stepped out from behind a parked truck. The cigarette dangling from the man's lips quivered and fell as his eyes shot open to saucers.

The first guard attempted to turn, but John pressed a hand on the man's back to keep him facing forward, and placed the fore end of his submachine gun on his right shoulder. Using the first guard as an impromptu weapon rest, he put a tight burst high into the second guard's chest.

As the approaching guard fell, John gave the other man a slight shove to create some space. The man rotated in slow motion as the ex-soldier pressed the trigger, letting the three-round burst ride up, starting near the guard's neck and ending just under one of his eyes.

John dropped to a combat crouch and swept his weapon across the area, making sure that no one else had heard the commotion. Satisfied that he was clear, he released the MP5's grip, letting it hang from the shoulder strap while he quickly pulled the two bodies back toward the tree line, dumping them into the ditch on the edge of the clearing.

Before heading back, John pulled out his KA-BAR, cut the shirt off one of the guards, and stuffed one end into his pocket before putting his knife away.

A large panel truck sat parked at the end of the parking area, backed into position and facing away from the compound. John crawled underneath and rolled over to his back, pulling out his knife. The blade made short work of the fuel lines.

He rolled out from underneath and reached the back of another car, stuffing the dead guard's shirt into the tailpipe. John's knife slid easily into the tires of the pickup truck and jeep parked farther down. Taking a few more minutes, John disabled more vehicles in essential positions to block in the rest or to make it difficult to get out without taking time to reposition.

With the first phase of his plan finished, John brought his suppressed MP5 back up and made his way to the most probable location to make his entry into the mansion, based on the discussions that he and Mark had about the satellite images. The layout of his chosen point of infiltration meant he could face more opposition, but it was the most likely location where they would be keeping his goddaughter.

* * *

Emily stepped out into the hallway, looking in both directions. With the guards gone, the whole area was quiet. *Empty.* Seizing the small window of opportunity, she padded her way to the farthest of the other two doors.

She pulled her lockpicks from her pocket, just in case she had to unlock the door. Holding the tools in one hand, Emily tucked the shard of broken plate under her arm and checked the knob. She heard someone approaching, and her heart raced. Relief washed over her as the unlocked door opened. She stepped inside just as the sentry crossed the end of the hall.

Like the room Warren had been keeping her in, this room was sparsely furnished, but her eyes lit up when she saw a laptop on the lone desk. Emily jogged over, her socks making little swishing sounds along the tiled floor.

The laptop felt heavy but very reassuring in her hands. She slid underneath the desk and lifted the display, powering the computer up. Even the relatively short boot-up time felt like an eternity to her. A rush of dizziness hit her as she thought about all the things that could go wrong. When the operating system came up, with a set of familiar icons on the desktop, Emily let out a breath.

Her finger glided along the trackpad, passing the cursor over each of the applications, looking for something suitable to send a message to someone. She opened the messaging app and logged the current user out, putting in her username and password to sign on.

The familiar chimes made her smile. She pulled up a new message, typed the username for her mom, and drafted a message. Emily didn't know where she was being held, but she told her mom about the kidnapping, her dad's being killed, and the details about the most significant people in the house, Warren, and Mr. Gordon.

She held her breath and hit Send.

* * *

Jennifer held the near-room-temperature cup of coffee in both hands, rocking her body back and forth. John had left almost an hour ago, and the lack of contact made her feel helpless. She kept her eyes fixed on the radio sitting on the table, resisting the urge to bombard John with constant questions.

She jumped up from her seat as her phone buzzed. Almost spilling her drink, she set the cup onto the table with shaky hands, rushing to pull her cell phone from her waistband where she kept it tucked. Her trembling fingers put in the four-digit code and saw the notification on the screen. Jennifer's mind had difficulty processing the message.

Her eyes bounced from the body of the message to the name of the sender. She wanted to read what it said, but her brain kept fixating on the sender's username. It was Emily!

The shout that escaped Jennifer's lips startled Parker, and his startled yell was almost as loud. She was both laughing and crying. Her words were indecipherable, and she kept waving the phone around.

"What is it?" Parker asked.

"It's Emily. She's alive!"

* * *

Tears streamed down Emily's face as she held her hands over her mouth. She read and reread the response from her mom.

Find a safe place to hide. Please don't take any unnecessary risks. Uncle John is coming to help you.

The rest was a nearly never ending stream of *I love you* and *Please stay safe.* Emily took several deep breaths, renewed with a sense of strength. *Uncle John* was her godfather. They weren't related, but he had been in the Army with her father.

She searched the desk for any other tools that would be useful but found nothing else. She walked to the window and opened the latch. It was unlocked, and she could open it from the inside.

* * *

The earpiece in John's ear crackled to life. He dropped to a crouch and swept the muzzle of his SMG across his field of view to make sure no one else posed a threat. He pressed his fingers on his radio to key the mic.

"Jennifer, calm down. I can't understand what you're saying." His voice was just above a whisper, but his words were transmitted loud and clear on the other end.

"Emily is alive. She just sent me a message."

157

John was almost surprised when the smile stretched across his face. He didn't expect the level of relief that hit him.

"That's great news," he said. "Keep me updated if you hear anything else."

"Okay, John. Thank you."

John stood up again and made his way to the compound's outer wall. He switched to the channel that he and Mark were using to coordinate his infiltration.

"Mark, are you there?"

"I'm here, John," Mark said. "What's your status?"

John filled Mark in on the situation, letting him know that of the six guards at his chosen point of infiltration, he had already eliminated three of them. He told Mark to limit radio contact but to call him if any significant changes occured.

John secured his weapons and took a short running start to leap up and grab the top of the wall at its shortest point. The cinder block scraped his fingers and palms, but he pulled himself up and over with ease.

The wall was meant as more of a deterrent than a fortification, and he was able to make it over without sacrificing stealth. He had to be careful not to kick off a firefight until he knew that Emily was safe.

John reached the corner of the building he and Mark had chosen as the best point of entry into the house and used his knife to pry a window open. He brought his MP5 back up and stepped inside, one leg at a time.

＊

Emily opened the window and leaned out. She was on the second floor, looking down at the 12-foot drop. The sun had gone down less than an hour ago, and the moon left the ground with patches of darkness where trees and shrubs cast heavy shadows.

Craning her neck out to either side, she spotted a drainpipe running along the corner of the building. She tried to stretch out to get a good hand hold on the pipe but found that it was out of reach. Emily knew that even with two good arms, it would be too difficult to climb down with the laptop.

She chewed on her lower lip for a minute, looking all around the window for anything that would help. A ledge-like trim ran along the outside below the window. It was broad enough for her toes or the edge of her foot, but not wide enough to walk along to reach the pipe.

Judging the distance, she figured that if she could hold on to the windowsill and stand on the tiny ledge, she could reduce the height of the drop enough to hit the ground without any major injuries.

Her broken arm throbbed in pain from the recent exertion. The thought of hitting the ground now scared her, but it was what she needed to do to get to safety. Her eye traveled up and down the curtains around the window, and an idea popped into her head.

She pulled one of the curtains tight on the rod and used the shard of the broken plate to cut rough strips out of it. A few minutes later, she had several scraps of the thick cloth, which she used to fashion a crude backpack, crossing the straps along the front of her body and pulling the computer close to her back. It didn't move much at all when she jostled around testing its fit.

It was now or never. Emily had to make her escape before the guards returned and realized she was gone. She lifted her left leg over the edge of the window and settled the inside edge of her foot on the small ledge. She held onto the windowsill and brought her right leg over, placing it in front of her left.

She crouched as low as possible, holding on to the window to keep from falling. While trying to slow her breathing, Emily spotted a guard patrolling the large backyard. Timing his route, she dropped to the ground while he had his back turned.

Emily's feet both hit the ground at almost the same time, compressing her whole body into a crouch and throwing her forward. Her body bounded ahead as she tried turning into a roll over her shoulder. Instead, she struck the ground hard on the elbow of her good arm.

She bit down on her lower lip hard to keep from crying out. The impact sent a wave of pain into her shoulder. She propped herself on her knees and tugged at the straps to make sure the laptop was still secure after her drop.

The guard turned, alerted by the sound she had made hitting the ground. Emily scrambled into the shadows, watching the man through the foliage as he visually scanned where she'd hit the ground. Tense seconds passed as he took a couple of steps forward, squinting and leaning to get a good look.

She held her breath up until the moment the man finally gave up his casual search and went back to his lazy route. She followed the bushes along the house until she reached a small clearing with a shed on the other side. Emily glanced back to the guard's route and saw that the way was clear.

CHAPTER

21

DAY 2   16:56   Mountain Time

"A View to a Kill"
Duran Duran

Mr. Gordon crested the top of the stairs and turned the corner to the hall, where he had locked Emily up. He looked down at his phone, checking to see if either of the men watching Jennifer had replied to his text. When he saw there were no new messages, his frustration rose.

I'll deal with those two later.

He looked up at the door and saw an empty chair where he had expected to see a guard posted. Gritting his teeth, Gordon covered the distance in hurried steps. He kicked the small wooden chair to one side and pushed the now unlocked door open. The empty room mocked him, as he saw only the unmade bed and a pair of girl's shoes.

The enforcer let out an angry growl as he headed to the bathroom to see if the guard had escorted their prisoner there. Again, he saw an empty room. Footsteps out in the hall pulled his attention back.

The guard who was supposed to be watching Emily stood, dumbfounded, as he looked down at the chair on the floor and the opened bedroom door. Gordon rushed him, driving a hand hard into the man's throat and pressing him up against the wall. His right hand pulled the pistol from the holster and pressed the muzzle against the guard's cheek.

"Where did she go!?"

Flecks of spittle peppered the panic-stricken face of the guard as he replied in a series of apologetic murmuring and shrugs. The urge to put a bullet into the incompetent soldier's brain was almost overwhelming. Gordon scowled, pulling in two deep breaths through flared nostrils before releasing his grip on the guard.

"Find her, now!" He grabbed the man by the collar and shoved him toward the stairs. "Sweep the area. Check every door. If you don't get her back in this room, I'll kill you myself."

He watched as the blubbering guard staggered away, clutching his hat and nodding.

*** *** ***

Inside the small, dusty shed, Emily closed the door, making sure to prevent any extra noise. She pulled the computer from her makeshift backpack and opened the display, watching as it woke again. Her eye reflexively dropped to the lower-right corner, showing that it still had a faint signal from her hiding spot.

It was weak, but the messaging app was still connected. Emily sent out a quick message, letting her mom know that she had found a good hiding spot in a shed tucked in the far corner of the property.

*** *** ***

Jennifer held her phone clutched in her hands, waiting for any communication from her daughter. Her heart soared when Emily's message came through. She was safe for now. Jennifer covered her mouth with one hand as tears of stress and joy streamed across her cheeks and fingers.

She put the phone down in her lap and picked the radio up from the couch cushion next to her. John needed to know where Emily was hiding. He needed to know that she was still alive and safe.

* * *

John moved to a dark corner and listened as footsteps clomped all around him. He could hear raised voices as people were running upstairs and through the hallway just outside the door where he was hiding.

Something must have alerted them, John thought. His first thought was that someone must have stumbled upon one of his earlier victims, or someone had failed to check in.

He reached up and unscrewed the light bulb from the lamp next to him and moved to the other side of the door. The guards were searching room by room, so it would be only a matter of time before someone reached him.

The doorknob rattled and slowly turned before a sliver of light from the hall spilled in from around the man at the entrance. An arm came in and flicked the light switch up. When nothing happened, the hand toggled the switch several more times.

The man huffed and sighed before stepping all the way in, heading for the far corner to start his search. John moved behind him and softly pushed the door shut. The ambient light faded as he wrapped a powerful arm around the guard's neck. John grabbed his other bicep, securing the chokehold, and hoisted the man off of his feet.

With a violent yank up and to one side, the man's neck snapped. John lowered the now limp body to the floor. In the moonlight, he could see that the uniform matched that of the rest of the soldiers he had already faced.

It wasn't until now that John noticed a resemblance to what he wore himself. The soldiers wore a dark gray uniform, but his black BDU pants and tactical vest looked similar enough especially with the assortment of military-grade firepower strapped to his body.

He crouched next to the body and pulled the hat from the dead man's head. John tested the fit, finding it a little tight. If he kept his movement casual to match that of the other mercenaries around him, he had a chance of passing as one of them.

John stepped out into the hall and moved toward the stairs, hugging the wall close. As he passed the last room, the door opened and a man stepped out. They bumped into each other, but as the man looked up, ready to utter a warning, John put a hand over the man's mouth and shoved him back into the room, following with his MP5 held close to his body.

Shooting from the hip, John unleashed a stream of bullets, stitching a short line from the man's diaphragm up to his left collar bone. The guard let out a short grunt of pain in his death throes.

More footsteps could be heard, moving frantically now. Even suppressed, the submachine gun's report would have been heard by people nearby. He risked sticking his head out into the hall to see if he had an opening to keep moving.

Two men hurried down the passage, pointed their weapons at him, and shouted commands to come out and surrender. John stepped back and shut the door, moving to the window as he heard multiple people radioing an intruder alert.

Looking out the window for a clear path to escape, John spotted a guard listening to his radio before visually scanning the house. He dropped back out of sight before the guard could spot him.

A firefight was inevitable now. John cursed to himself and took up a combat position, executing a tactical reload to top off his MP5. He covered the door and chose a location that let him control his angle of fire to prevent the bullets from going farther into the house. He couldn't risk hitting Emily if she was nearby.

His silent approach seemingly gone, he turned the stolen radio on to listen. The radio chatter multiplied as men radioed their fighting positions. John heard a familiar voice among the mercenaries shouting tactical information. He realized that he still had his earpiccc in, and Jennifer's voice was trying to break through.

John turned the stolen radio's volume down and switched to an open channel on his radio, so Mark could also monitor this conversation with Jennifer.

"Repeat that," he said, no longer whispering into his throat mic.

"Emily is still alive," Jennifer said. "She's safe, hiding in a shed in a far corner of the property."

"Mark, did you get all that?"

"I've got the location of the shed, John," Mark said. "She's on the far corner of the property from your position."

John looked at the incoming data on his phone, showing his location, in relation to the shed where Emily was hiding. He would be able to cover the ground much faster outside, but with his position compromised, the lack of cover was too much of a risk. He would have to fight his way *through* the house.

CHAPTER

22

DAY 2   17:14 Mountain Time

"Fight For Your Right"
Beastie Boys

With his position compromised, John slung the H&K MP5 and switched to the M4 carbine. His M4 didn't have a sound suppressor like the submachine gun, but he didn't need to sneak around anymore. He would also need the added firepower now.

The men outside radioed his position, organizing their approach. They moved and sounded like professionals, but John pulled his door open and engaged them first. They wouldn't be prepared for his direct approach.

He brought the muzzle of his weapon around to where he knew the incoming soldiers would position themselves for entry. The rifle spit thunder and lead, dropping the two men approaching the door.

John stepped out just as a third man rounded the corner with his M4 carbine shouldered, returning fire. John was forced to dart across the hall and slip into a different room to avoid the onslaught.

* * *

The call came in about the intruder as Mr. Gordon stepped into a home office at the end of the hall, near Emily's room. He approached the open window, seeing the scraps of curtain fabric on the ground. He crouched and picked up a length of the cloth.

Did she use this to climb out?

He stood and leaned out the window, looking for any evidence that the girl had used the curtain to climb down. In the faint light he could see some rough gouges in the grass below but no other signs of Emily.

Gordon scanned the property, putting himself into the mindset of a captive trying to escape. The shed on the far end caught his eye. In the girl's position, he would consider that a good hiding spot until the chance for a full escape presented itself.

The enforcer checked to make sure all of his weapons were secure, planning to leap down from the window and check the shed for their escaped prisoner.

He phased out the desperate radio chatter and placed a palm on the windowsill, ready to climb out. Before he could get a leg out, fully automatic gunfire chattered from the other end of the house.

With his reflexes kicking into overdrive, Gordon ran straight for the door, pulling his pistol and stepping out. He dashed to the far end of the upstairs floor and barged into Warren Ratcliffe's office, unannounced. Warren had also heard the gunfire and looked to his enforcer with worry and surprise on his face.

Several security men rushed by to the stairs, not sure of what was happening. Another guard ran by, following the others. Gordon grabbed the man by the sleeve and pulled him into the office.

"Get a team to escort Mr. Ratcliffe out of here. Radio for the transport to meet him at the secure back exit," Gordon said.

The man nodded and spoke quickly into his radio.

Mr. Gordon took out his radio and called for status updates. He needed to know just how large a force they were dealing with, and what directions they were attacking from. The response was confusing.

171

Only one confirmed the sighting so far, and it had been inside the house.

"Sir," the guard in the room said. "The vehicles have been compromised. No ground transport is available."

Jesus, what is happening? Mr. Gordon thought.

Changing his plan, he said to the guard, "Go get the Juggernaut."

The man's only reply was a wide-eyed look of awe and apprehension.

He grabbed a handful of the man's lapel and jabbed him in the chest with his pistol to emphasize every few words.

"Get to the armory, and put on the Juggernaut," he said before pushing the man away. "I'll arrange for the helicopter to pick Mr. Ratcliffe up on the roof. Guard the main entrance until he gets out safely."

* * *

John leaned out from the room and fired two bursts, forcing the man back behind cover. He stepped out and moved forward, maintaining his aggression. His opponent leaned out, aiming at the door, clear of where John was standing.

John fired a longer burst with the M4 through the corner the man was using for cover. A few of the

5.56mm rounds managed to punch through the drywall and two-by-four studs, scoring center mass shots.

He turned the corner, past the fallen soldier and saw two more men standing at the far end of the hall, ready for battle. They flinched as he emptied the rest of the magazine, firing the rifle from his hip. When the M4's hammer clicked on an empty chamber, John wasted no time, letting the weapon drop on its sling and pulling his 1911 pistol with a smooth draw stroke. Two .45 caliber slugs punched holes through the first man's heart before he could react.

John walked forward, shifting his front sight to the second man. The soldier aimed his rifle as the pistol cracked two more times. John followed the double tap to his target's chest with a third shot between the eyes, taking him off his feet. He reached the two bodies and put one more round in the first man before reloading his pistol.

Shouting voices approached from the other end of the hall. John spun around, putting his back to the wall and firing his handgun with one hand. They answered back with rifle fire. John turned the knob of the nearest door and shouldered his way in while firing until his pistol locked open.

Footsteps approached cautiously, and John could hear quiet voices just outside the door. He reloaded his Colt 1911 pistol and slipped it back into the holster. Before he could reload his M4 carbine, he heard one of the men say, "Frag it." John knew this meant someone was going to throw a fragmentation grenade into the room to clear it before they moved in to finish him. There were no other exits, so John had to do something they wouldn't expect if he wanted any chance of surviving this. He moved to the door and stacked himself against the wall.

The doorknob twisted quietly and smoothly, and the door flew open. John saw an arm swing in and throw the grenade, and snatched the wrist with a powerful grip before the man could pull his hand back out. He grunted with effort and yanked on the arm, sending the arm and its owner sailing through the air into the middle of the room.

In the next instant, John crouched and used his powerful legs to launch himself into a dive through the doorway. He turned in midair, landing on his left side as his back smashed into the wall across the hallway.

The two men remaining outside were crouched in anticipation of the grenade blast until they heard a scream coming from inside the room. They realized with a shock that their target was outside the room, while one of their own was now inside. John lifted his H&K and fired from his back at the closer of the two men. The MP5 coughed, and 9mm rounds tore through flesh and bone. The remaining man brought his rifle up, taking aim at John.

The sudden explosion from the grenade threw the rifleman's aim off. John rolled away from the far wall as bullets stitched the floor next to him. He stopped on his back and unloaded his submachine gun into the final gunman. The barrage threw the soldier against the wall before he crumpled to the floor.

John thumbed the release and yanked the magazine free. He grabbed a fresh mag and slammed it into the H&K just as the man hit the ground.

With the final gunshot still echoing, John had a moment to reload his M4 carbine and do a quick search of the dead men, finding two extra M4 magazines and a grenade, before he left the area ahead of the footsteps running in his direction.

* * *

"Just a sec," Mark said, cradling the handset of his desk phone on his shoulder while typing out an email on his laptop.

He put the call on hold and focused on making his message as clear as possible before hitting Send. He could hear the swoosh of the email application, letting him know the message had been sent as he picked the call back up.

"I said I need you to keep the police back." He listened to the incredulous reply before upping the aggressive tone. "Look, I could just pull rank, but you know you owe me a favor, and I'm calling it in right now. Keep all local law enforcement outside of my operation."

After John's mission had escalated to a full-on firefight, Mark had been scrambling to make all the necessary calls to explain the situation to his superiors, call in some support for John, and keep all other variables in check.

"I'll give you the all clear as soon as my man is ready for support. Until then, you will stand down," Mark said before hanging up the phone.

John, if you make it out of this, you owe me a beer.

CHAPTER

23

"Ace of Spades"
Motörhead

John moved quickly to keep distance between himself and his pursuers. He rounded the corner of a short corridor that led to the main hallway, which would take him to the other side of the mansion.

The moment he stepped into the main hallway, he saw a man in the wrong time period. A soldier, wearing what looked at first like a heavy suit of medieval armor, was holding an AK-47 and standing in the middle of the path. John then noticed the more modern look of the soldier's armored suit. It resembled a dark metallic version of a bomb disposal outfit. John saw letters stenciled across the front: *Juggernaut Prototype*.

The soldier in the Juggernaut suit was facing the front door when he noticed John. He pivoted his armored bulk to square up with the new threat down the hall.

John's M4 rifle was coming up to fire at the same time as the armored man's AK. It was then that another shocking realization flew through John's mind at lightning speed. What he had thought was an AK-47 was fitted with a larger barrel than the rifle normally had. The drum magazine that stuck out of the bottom, already intimidating on its own, was also thicker than usual. John was face-to-barrel with the Saiga-12, a semiautomatic shotgun built on the legendary AK 47 platform.

Even though the metallic monster had the rifle up and ready, John's reflexes were quicker. He brought the M4 to his hip and fired a long burst into the man blocking his path. The bullets sparked and bounced off the armor, inflicting no visible damage at all. The Saiga-12 roared and released a series of rapid-fire booms. John pivoted away and retreated around the corner, but not before a shotgun blast slammed into the front plate of his tactical vest, his rifle partially absorbing some of the impact.

He nearly fell before making it back around the corner. Sections of the back wall disintegrated as the burst tracked John, destroying a large part of the structure.

That confirmed another worry he had. Since it was built similarly to an AK-47, it was relatively straightforward for a trained gunsmith to convert the Saiga-12 to fully automatic, making it capable of firing 600 rounds of 12-gauge ammunition per minute.

John had the wind knocked out of him from the hit he had taken. At such a close range, the buckshot was still in a tight enough pattern for the tac vest to catch all of the pellets, but that only meant he had suffered the full force of a 12-gauge shotgun blast to his body.

He turned and staggered back the way he had come, as three men moved toward him from the opposite end of that short corridor. John moved toward them and fired his carbine, hoping an aggressive tactic would give him a psychological advantage, causing them to retreat.

The M4 fired only a single round, striking the lead man in the neck, then fell silent. John instinctively performed a lightning-fast reload, but the carbine failed to fire again. The shotgun blast that had hit his M4 must have damaged it.

The two remaining mercenaries fired back, one with a pistol and the other with an AK-47. John had no choice now but to head back in the direction of the buckshot-breathing dragon.

John recalled a small section of the hallway with an open doorway leading into another room that he had seen when first entering the main hall. It had been on his left when he faced the Juggernaut and halfway between the two of them.

He turned and sprinted, zigzagging to avoid the gunfire following him, and rounded the corner at full speed. The Saiga was already aimed at John as he entered the hall, but his speed made him difficult to track. John covered the last 5 feet to the entryway. The shotgun started its fearsome roar as he leaped through the opening.

He crashed through a small glass table and onto the floor. The shards cut into him, but the pain wasn't even a blip on his mental radar as he scrambled away from the gunfire punching through the wall.

John saw he was in a den, furnished as an office. He crawled to the closest corner of the room as the two men reached the doorway and fired blindly into the den. The shotgun ripped holes through the wall, and a ricochet from the AK-47 struck his thigh. John sprayed his MP5 through the barrier, trying to get his opponents to take cover. He rolled behind the desk amid the rain of wood, lead, and glass. There was a lull in the shooting as the soldiers approached outside the room. John caught a small glimpse of the gunmen through missing sections of the drywall.

He dropped the empty magazine from the H&K and reloaded it with the partially full magazine he had replaced earlier. This one had fewer than ten rounds left. John took the frag grenade off his vest, and pulled the pin, still holding the spoon tight to its side, keeping the explosive from arming itself. He emptied the MP5 at the opening, forcing the two men to step away from it. Once the submachine gun ran dry, John scrambled to the wall.

He held the grenade in his tightly clenched left fist and punched directly through the den wall, into the hallway. John dropped the grenade on the other side and pulled his arm back. More gunfire greeted him near where his fist had punched through, and he lunged back under the desk, pulling the big office chair in front for any bit of cover he could get. The man in the Juggernaut realized too late what was happening.

He yelled a warning through his armored helmet, "Grena—"

The explosion overpowered every other sound in the room. The blast shredded the wall between them. The blast wave shoved John and the desk back a couple of feet, and a bit of shrapnel punched into the side of his vest, penetrating the thinner protective material at that point. Another grazed John on the side of his head, causing him to black out for a moment.

He snapped awake and saw that smoke and dust had filled the room. His ears were ringing, and blood flowed down from his nose, soaking his mustache. He was disoriented, but he drove his heavily muscled frame forward, nearly on pure instinct, and smashed through the hole where the grenade had exploded.

John fell to the floor on the other side, next to the now dead armored man. The two other men, also hurt from the grenade blast, started getting back to their feet. John scooped up the automatic Saiga-12 and fired at the soldiers as they brought their guns up. The 00-buckshot storm took them off their feet and sent them to meet their respective makers.

John pulled a fresh drum magazine from a belt of drums on the Juggernaut and reloaded the shotgun. He dropped the MP5 and M4 carbine to the floor, and attached two more drum magazines to his tactical vest wherever he could. John limped down the long hallway, toward the other end of the mansion. Once there, he would fight his way outside and to the shed where Emily was hiding. He would get to her. He would protect her.

*** * ***

John took a mental inventory of his injuries, to assess his situation. He could deal with the various small cuts and scrapes. The shotgun blast to the chest had bruised, or possibly cracked, one of his ribs. His breathing was pained and shallow. The wound in his right thigh, from the ricochet, was bleeding, but it hadn't penetrated too deeply or come near an artery. The shrapnel in his right side was also not too deep, having been slowed some by the vest.

He kept pressure on the wound by pressing the stock of the Saiga-12 automatic 12-gauge shotgun firmly to his side. Blood dripped from his nose, head, and one of his ears. The ringing sound would make it difficult for John to hear someone coming, so he had to remain extra vigilant.

Moving through the hallway, John walked right down the center, no longer traveling along either of the walls. His posture and stride were high and deliberate, ready for any head-to-head confrontation.

As he made it into a larger opening, boots pounded on the hardwood steps as a soldier came running down, firing his rifle as he moved. John turned to his right and met the man's rush with a three shot burst, sending a fusillade of 00-buckshot that threw his target's body backward onto the stairs.

Another door burst open as a mercenary stepped out, not sure where his threat was. He faced John with his M4 aiming at the ground. For a split second, John could see the process in the man's eyes. He wanted to bring the weapon up to fire on the intruder, but it was clear that it was already too late. The man turned to flee. After two steps, the Saiga-12 hammered five shots in rapid succession, cutting the soldier down in an instant.

Reaching the room the soldier had just come from, John kept the weapon pressed at his hip and swept the muzzle through. At the far end, a set of French double doors opened out into the backyard. John mapped out his path in his mind, assuring himself that the shed where Emily was hiding wasn't too far away.

He stepped through the doors onto a large covered patio running the length of that section of the house. A series of heavy concrete pillars provided support for the roof. Moving through the yard, John saw three men taking cover and aiming their weapons at him.

The bright muzzle flashes kicked him into action. The barely audible reports from their rifles pierced the ringing in his ears, but he had difficulty figuring out their firing and reloading patterns. John used the patio's pillars as cover to reload, moving forward with a series of bursts from his 12-gauge assault rifle.

The first man screamed in agony as 00-buckshot shredded the wood-and-wrought-iron bench he was using as cover. Another soldier took two shotgun blasts dead center as he tried to move up for a better angle of attack.

As John's burst made short work of that man, the last merc propped his weapon against the short wall he was hiding behind and dumped an entire magazine at the pillar John was using for cover. Before he could drop back, one of the rounds struck the concrete nearby, sending a spray of dust and debris peppering John's eyes. He blinked as the stinging caused him to drop down and get out of the line of sight.

The soldier jumped up to his feet and fled, letting his empty rifle clatter at his feet. John leaned out in a crouch and fired the Saiga-12, struggling to get a good sight picture through blurred vision and watery eyes, until the magazine ran out of ammo. He dropped the now empty shotgun and pulled the 1911 from the drop leg holster, stepping out from cover to head   for   the   shed.

CHAPTER
24

DAY 2   18:11 Mountain Time

"Seek and Destroy"
  Metallica

Mr. Gordon stepped out at the opposite side of the lush backyard, making visual contact with the intruder. One man, sent by an unknown player, was apparently the cause of the death and destruction that had occurred today. This man would ultimately fail in his mission to get his hands on the encryption device. Gordon had seen to that when he secured the roof and arranged for the safe extraction of his client, Warren Ratcliffe. The giant bloodied stranger was turning back to face the mansion when he heard the thrumming blades of the approaching transport.

A Bell 222 helicopter touched down on the roof, bouncing on the wheeled gears from a hurried landing. A man in a suit carrying a briefcase climbed aboard and slammed the door closed behind him.

"It's too late," Gordon called out from across the lawn, raising his voice to carry over the thumping of the rotors.

The mystery man whipped his head toward the speaker. The two combatants couldn't be more visually different. Mr. Gordon draped his cream-colored suit jacket on a lawn chair and rolled up the sleeves of his turquoise dress shirt. His always creased slacks hung on him in perfectly straight lines, ending at modified dress shoes designed to give him traction for a fight. The unknown soldier approaching him was a battered and bleeding mess, holding a 1911 semiautomatic pistol. The man was a relic from an ancient war.

Gordon stood with his feet casually close together and his hands raised out to his sides. A Kydex hard-shell holster sat tucked inside his waistband in the *one o'clock appendix carry* position. The custom stippled grip of a Glock 19 was poking out, opposite of the pouches holding three spare magazines. The Bell helicopter rose above the highest point of the mansion's roof and flew away.

"It's over," he said, satisfied that this intruder had failed in his mission. "You won't catch him, now, my friend."

Warren had the prototype decryption device in his possession, and he was now on his way to a secure location. Gordon's remaining task was to kill this man and clean up the mess.

The bloody intruder gripped the Colt tightly in his fist and turned to face him head-on. Gordon's hands were still held out to his sides, and his fingers twitched slightly. The moment of stillness carried on for an eternity and then was shattered in a flash. The mystery man raised his pistol, and Gordon's hand snatched the Glock out of the holster in a blur of movement.

Both men were experienced gunfighters. They shot while moving to any cover they could find in this serene landscape-turned-war-zone. Ratcliffe's security specialist moved sideways, attempting to flank his target. He noticed that the intruder chose to advance with aggression, moving forward to seek cover.

He wants to close the distance. He's making it too easy for me to circle him.

He almost pitied this man, like a matador about to destroy a bull. Mr. Gordon crouched behind an ornate Greek statue of a beautiful woman. He fired three shots at the intruder, almost steering his opponent. The only viable cover for the man-bull rushing forward was the small fountain between the two men.

He would drive the soldier toward the fountain with well-placed gunfire, then continue to flank his prey for the finishing shot. Just as he was brining the Glock up, a burst of .45 caliber slugs punched through the edge of the statue at one of the weak points. One of the heavy 230-grain rounds drilled him low to the left of his sternum. His concealed body armor caught the bullet, but the air hissed from Mr. Gordon's lungs as he spiraled to the ground.

Was that luck or skill? he thought. Getting his breath back, Mr. Gordon smiled slightly at the thought of facing a worthy opponent. He had to move quickly and force the man behind the fountain to maintain his original plan. He leaned out from behind the statue while on his back, but he lost sight of his prey.

He triggered a burst of suppressing fire in the area where the man would most likely be, then rolled to a crouch and continued to move.

* * *

John found himself in a gunfight with a man who had chosen to announce his presence instead of shooting John in the back. This man wanted a fair fight, which made this foe either very dangerous or very foolish.

Regardless, John needed to end the fight quickly. He was down to the last magazine for his pistol, having emptied his weapon to close the distance to this man.

His opponent's Glock 19 had a capacity of 15 rounds of 9mm bullets in the mag plus one in the chamber. With the three reloads on his opponent's belt, this skilled fighter had started with at least 60 rounds. John was down to seven.

He pressed his shoulder behind a short garden wall and saw his opponent take cover behind a statue. The man's plan seemed to be to use strategic fire to force John to move forward behind the fountain. That would open John up to a flanking attack. It was a solid plan that he would have employed himself if the roles were reversed.

John's next maneuver would be the most dangerous. He sighted his Colt semiautomatic on his opponent's cover and saw the man raise his pistol. He fired at his target through the more delicate parts of the statue, confident that the heavy slugs would penetrate the material.

He saw the man go down in a spray of stone chunks and dust. Seizing his opening, John leaped over the wall and headed for the fountain, firing the last of his ammo to cover his movement. The slide locked back, and John dropped the pistol. His left foot dug hard into the soft lawn as he switched directions, sprinting toward the gunman. He moved to his right, using the statue to hide his approach.

John seized his only chance to reach his foe and change the rules of the fight. Hand-to-hand range didn't make his opponent's gun any less dangerous, but without a firearm of his own, any distance between them would mean John was out of the fight completely.

His wounds sent sharp signals of pain and his heart hammered in his chest as his boots churned the ground with each determined step.

* * *

Mr. Gordon launched from a crouching position to continue his flanking maneuver. The instant he broke cover, he found the giant of a man bearing down on him at a full run. The sudden appearance of his opponent caught him completely off guard.

Not a man to be shaken easily, the mercenary swung his pistol up to shoot the charging bull. A huge paw of a hand swatted the gun to the side as 240 pounds of focused mass took him completely off his feet.

The two hit the ground together, and the brute attempted to pin Gordon with his weight while throwing massive fists to his body and head, with frightening accuracy. Any ordinary man would have been overwhelmed by the sheer size of the assailant and the ferocity of his attack.

But Gordon was highly trained to fight from any position. He pulled his opponent close to minimize the damage until he could find a stable enough base to create some distance.

He shifted his hips out from underneath his opponent and wedged his knee on the big man's hip. Mr. Gordon reached back to the sheath attached to his belt, wrapping a hand around the grip. He shifted again, bringing his other foot up, and kicked away to make some space as he deployed the knife from his back with a quick swipe.

His opponent leaned back to avoid the blade. Gordon rolled away and stood. He studied the mystery man, impressed by the skill he had showed during the gunfight. Admittedly, gunplay was the weakest part of his skill set, and he conceded the win to his opponent.

Now it was a different story, as Gordon brought his tactical folding knife into a fighting position. The man-bull reached to a sheath on his thigh and drew a large knife of his own. *The bull has a sword,* Mr. Gordon thought, amused again. Close-quarters combat was where he was the most formidable, and his blade whirled in a hypnotizing pattern, looking for blood.

***

John held his knife ready as his opponent moved in. The two combatants exchanged a series of slashes and stabs, neither scoring a hit. It was only a matter of time before this dangerous man would land a significant strike on John.

The movements of the smaller tactical knife were quick and confusing as they searched for contact. Only the large size of his knife and reluctance to overcommit to any attacks kept John from any further injury. The man in front of him was much faster and very experienced with a blade.

John saw an opening as his opponent stepped in too far, missing a lunge meant for a space between his ribs. He counter-stabbed with his KA-BAR and realized too late that he had made a mistake. The attack had been a feint and he had drawn John right into a trap.

The knife fighter controlled the big blade by clamping the fingers and palm of his free hand over the back of the spine. A quick underhand slash caught John along the back of his hand, and he instinctively lost his grip on the blade.

The smaller knife continued to arc away from him, and then circled back looking to sink into the side of John's neck. He brought his left arm up at the last moment to shield himself from the killing blow. The blade drove through his forearm, and the tip poked out through the other side.

John grunted as the pain sensors in his mind went into overload. He hooked his right hand around the back of the man's head and drove the top of his forehead into his opponent's face. The vicious headbutt smashed cartilage and cracked bone. The man released the grip on his knife and dropped John's KA-BAR to the ground. His foe fell back, blood spraying from his nose, but managed to roll over his shoulder and end up on his feet again.

John swept the big knife to the side with one large boot and gripped the handle of the tactical blade buried in his arm, pulling it free, with a growl. He saw the dangerous man adjust his stance, preparing to fight bare-handed against a knife. Keeping eye contact, John deliberately threw the knife away.

He knew it could be a huge mistake to do this, especially considering he was already severely injured and now bleeding from a new wound. His opponent hadn't shot him in the back when he had the chance. John's gesture was a show of respect between two warriors.

The fighter standing before him had proven to be much faster, and possibly more skilled. While John's tactical vest would help absorb some of his opponent's strikes, he would eventually be overwhelmed by the experienced attacker, as well as by his injuries. John unfastened the buckles and the hook-and-loop closures. He took the protective vest off, trading the defense it offered for a bit more mobility.

The man waited for John to remove his body armor but lunged the moment it hit the ground. The fighter's movements were fast and surgical. The attacks came from varying angles, delivered by hands and elbows, feet and knees. John's counterattacks were blocked or deflected with skilled precision. He was being picked apart by a better fighter.

The uneven exchange continued for another three and a half minutes, until his opponent landed a roundhouse kick right on the gunshot wound on John's leg. The attack sent John down to a knee, hands on the ground. He was beaten and exhausted. His opponent stalked forward and stopped before delivering what would likely be a killing blow.

"For what it's worth, you were a worthy opponent," the man said, preparing to end the battle.

John stayed on a knee but straightened up, looking his opponent in the eye. The man brought his knee up, chambering the leg to drive it into John's neck.

His foot fired out but just missed when John leaned back and thrust one of his boots into the supporting knee of his opponent.

The sickening crack of bones, cartilage, and ligaments reverberated through the boot. The mercenary let out a short, pained yell and collapsed to the ground. John rose to his feet and pulled the smaller man up to a standing position.

The fighter lashed out with a right hook, but John easily deflected it. He scooped the man up and lifted him high into the air. John dropped his weight to one knee and brought his opponent crashing down, spine first, onto the other knee. Vertebrae cracked and shattered, and John dropped the wrecked body to the floor. Rising with pained effort, John stood and took two steps toward the shed, where Emily was waiting.

Groaning in barely contained agony, the man turned his head to face John.

He asked, in ragged breaths and through gritted teeth, "Wh-who… sent you?"

John stopped, his back still turned, and stood silent for a moment.

"The girl," he said, and continued walking.

CHAPTER

25

DAY 2   18:40 Mountain Time

"Meet Me Halfway"
Kenny Loggins

John grunted in pain as he reached up for the shed's handle. He pulled the wooden door open and stepped into the entry.

"Emily?" His throat ached, making his voice more of a croak. "Are you in here?"

He let his eyes adjust to the dark searching the small room for his goddaughter. A small figure peered out from the shadows, stepping forward.

"Uncle John!" Emily ran to him.

Even in the dim light, he could see the glint of the tears on her face. She ran into his arms and clutched his body tightly around his injured ribs. He suppressed a groan and held her as well, slowly tightening his embrace as the pain gradually melted away. He felt himself wrapping around her, wanting to protect her from any more danger in the world.

"C'mon, kid. Let's get you home to your mother."

John pushed himself back to his feet and held Emily's hand, leading her out of the shed. He heard sirens approaching. The flashing lights danced along the yard and driveway as police came pouring out of their vehicles.

"Put your hands up!" one of the officers ordered, as at least a dozen more trained their pistols and shotguns on John and Emily.

"Let her go now," another officer said.

John ushered Emily protectively behind him. He considered the possibility that these police officers might also be corrupt, and his mind was putting a battle plan together.

A tiny hand wrapped around his wrist and tugged down.

"Please, Uncle John. Just listen to them. I promise we'll be okay."

He looked down into her eyes, and nodded. The rush of adrenaline was finally wearing off at that moment. His body almost collapsed under its weight as he lowered himself to his knees and laced his fingers behind his head.

Four officers approached with weapons drawn. One knelt down to pick Emily up, carrying her back to the safety of the patrol cars. Two more kept their guns up as the last officer stepped behind John and secured his hands behind his back with a pair of cuffs.

The lights flooded his vision, and all sound faded into the background as fatigue took over.

EPILOGUE

DAY 3   00:44   Mountain Time

"Top Gun Anthem"
Harold Faltermeyer

It was past midnight, and the police presence had increased. So far only two other men had been found alive: an unarmed mercenary running through the lawn into a group of police, and a second man in the backyard with a shattered spine.

A pair of officers had cuffed John Stone to an unpadded steel bench in the back of a police van. The officers on scene were still not sure entirely what had happened here, and didn't want to take any chances. The medics had to tend to John's injuries while he sat restrained in the van.

Before the double doors in the back swung closed, John spotted an all-black SUV pulling up to the scene. It didn't match the look of any local police vehicles. Federal agencies had just arrived, and a battle for jurisdiction was about to start.

John tested the cuffs' fit, circling his wrists and wiggling his fingers to get as comfortable as he could, settling in for the long haul. After a few minutes, one of the van's back doors swung open and a well-dressed man stepped inside. At first glance, his demeanor screamed *federal agent,* but John noticed that the color and cut of his suit weren't part of any government standards he had seen.

He looked the newcomer in the eye, and a hint of recognition hit him. John didn't know him personally but had a vague sense that he knew who the man was. Skipping all formal introductions, the man took his sunglasses off and slid them into the inner pocket of his jacket.

"Mr. Stone, I won't waste your time," he said with a smooth, confident tone. "I'm putting a team together and—"

"I'm retired." John cut him off.

The man smiled and nodded. "Yes, we know, but you'll want to hear my offer."

John stared into the man's eyes, looking for any sign that this might be a set-up of some kind. He saw only the resolve and determination of someone who stood behind his words.

"Alright, you've got my attention," John said.

"Like I said, I'm putting a team together. A group of individuals with varied specialties that can fill many needs."

The man readjusted, smoothing out the pant legs of his slacks, and sat in front of John. He continued in a lower voice.

"Warren Ratcliffe, the gentleman who fled the scene in a helicopter a few hours ago, is part of a new breed of bad guys," he said. "We need a task force that can function on a different level with a method of operations not seen in government agencies today."

"Outside of the typical military chain of command," John said, finishing the man's statement.

"You see exactly where I'm going with this, then." He handed John a business card.

John looked down at the card and looked back up at the man with a smirk. The mystery man chuckled, pulled a set of keys from his pocket, and removed the handcuffs. John held the card between his thumb and index finger, looking it over. Plain white stock with only a single phone number, starting with a Washington, D.C., area code.

The man held the cuffs up, dangling from a thumb. "If you're wondering what's on the table, I can guarantee you a full pardon of all crimes. You knew that your vigilante one-man army raid was going to land you behind bars, but my guess is that you didn't care."

John lifted his eyes from the card. Going into his assault, he hadn't expected to make it out unscathed, but the possibility of death or ending up behind bars had taken a back seat to making sure that Emily made it out safe.

"I'll give you some time to think about it, Mr. Stone. Call me when you've decided," the man said.

John slid the card into his back pocket, then looked him directly in the eyes.

"When do we start?"

JOHN   STONE   WILL   RETURN

DID YOU LIKE THIS BOOK?

Leave a review on Amazon and let us know! It only takes a moment and helps us, as independent authors, tremendously.

In our schedule of books, we have a ton of different ideas we would like to work on, but if you loved reading about John Stone, and want us to continue to tell his story, you, as the reader, can let us know directly. It is very difficult for us to get an idea of which books work without that feedback.

Let others know about it as well, and encourage them to leave a review. Right now, our future releases are all based on reader feedback, so if we don't know you liked the book, future sequels will sit in the queue along with the rest.

Thank you in advance!
The   Manning   Brothers

Want more of John Stone?

Here's a sneak peek of Divide and Conquer

CHAPTER

1

A harsh bluish-white glow from the LED streetlights blended with the soft radiance of the half moon, casting sharp shadows along the entrance of a fenced in the building nestled along a low-traffic street in Las Vegas' North side. A service van approached the small booth at the front gate, manned by an unassuming guard.

The man checked his watch and stood, approaching the driver side window. "Can I help you?"

"Delivery," the driver said, glancing to the side with a folded piece of paper pinched between his fingers.

The guard reached out to grab the document, and the van's side door slid open. He turned his head, shocked at what he saw, and dropped his hand to the pistol on his belt.

The driver pulled a Soviet PB suppressed pistol, pointed the muzzle at the guard's head, and fired. The handgun let out a *CHOK* as the heavy subsonic bullet buried itself into his skull. A second man caught the guard's crumpling body, pulling him into the opened van door. A third stepped out, wearing the same uniform as the guard, straightening his tie and adjusting his hat. He plucked the dead guard's ID card from his shirt and strolled over to the guard booth, swiping the stolen credentials into an electronic reader to open the gate.

Without a word, the driver gave the new guard a nod, rolling his window up and bringing the van through the gate.

The man at the gate returned the gesture with a casual salute using the key card and tossed it back through the van's side door before it slammed shut.

The van pulled through the parking lot and stopped near the side of the building. Two men that looked like the tactical equivalent of *The Odd Couple* hopped out. Both wore dark blue, heavy-duty coveralls, but one man was freshly shaven, his short hair well-groomed and parted on one side. The other had a baseball cap pulled over his unruly hair, and a dark, bushy beard. They headed to the side entrance, looked to either side and then peered through the narrow vertical glass before the man swiped the guard's access card. A buzz echoed through the mostly empty hall as the electronic lock clicked, releasing the latch. The two walked down the hall, passing an oblivious employee who barely gave the pair of blue-collar workers a second glance.

They reached a secure area, swiping the credentials again to gain access, and headed for the surveillance room. At the keypad, well-groomed man knelt and dropped a bag of tools, digging inside. Bearded man pulled out a phone, pretending to check up on social media. The two, posing as technicians called in to fix a faulty access point, hid in plain sight, cracking the lock to access the data inside. The keypad let out a beep and click, and the two slipped in securing the door behind them.

They spent a few minutes getting familiar with the layout of the room, examining the monitors, and racks of humming computers used to store hours of high def video from the security cameras. Bearded man pointed to the control console with two fingers, then headed to a patch panel on the back wall. Well-groomed man nodded and pulled an ultraportable laptop from his pack, plugging it directly into the boards controlling the security system.

The door beeped and opened, air hissing out of the climate controlled room. A man in uniform stepped in. He scanned the room and cast a cautious gaze at the two workers inside. He held a small flashlight in an icepick grip at shoulder height, pointing the 400-lumen beam at the strangers in utility garb. He squinted and ran his tongue along his bottom lip.

"What's going on here?" he asked, thumb hooked into his belt, just forward of a holstered Smith & Wesson M&P.

"Work order," bearded man said, walking over from the panel. He glanced over the guard's shoulder to the door, then continued. "Your security system was on the fritz, and we got the call to come out here as soon as our shift started." He spoke in a slight accent the guard couldn't exactly place.

The security guard looked back and forth at the two, then down at his wristwatch. "Little late for a maintenance call, isn't it? I'm going to need to see your work order."

The man chuckled. "Yeah, I figured you would. Just doing your job too, huh?" He stepped forward, reaching one hand into the pocket of his coveralls. Now the guard recognized the accent. It was Russian.

The bearded repairman pulled the PB pistol from his pocket and leveled it at the guard in a smooth motion. His movements remained casual, and the smile never left his face. The dichotomy of his action and his intent caused the guard to hesitate. *CHOK CHOK*

The man fired twice into the guard's face and kept an eye on the door as he collapsed to the ground. The guard convulsed, eyes wide with shock, and died where he lay.

Well-groomed man never stopped typing at his keyboard during the whole exchange. Bearded man dragged the guard's body into a far corner, out of sight of anyone walking into the room. After that, he finished his task of splicing wires together at the panel.

"I'm good here. You've got access now," bearded man said, dropping his tools back into the bag and pulling out a 9A-91 carbine. He affixed a suppressor to the muzzle and snapped the shoulder stock open.

His teammate entered a series of keystrokes on the laptop, watching several progress bars whip by before the screen rewarded him with a confirmation that he had control of the security system. He pulled a radio from his left pocket and thumbed the button to transmit.

"We're in," well-groomed man said, speaking Russian.

He clicked several options on the screen, and the front door unlocked, while all exterior doors throughout the facility went on lockdown.

He watched a monitor showing their van outside. A group of four, dressed in all black and carrying short-barreled, suppressed 9A-91 assault carbines stepped out of the vehicle and moved to the front entrance in formation. The hacker scanned the wall of monitors until he found the corridor he was looking for. Thumbing the radio again, he called out the location to the team outside, directing them to the Data Storage wing. With a quick keyboard shortcut, the primary display showed a high definition camera feed of the group outside, stacked at the entrance. Once all four were in position, the team leader looked up at the camera and gave a signal. Well-groomed man nodded, and bearded man flipped a switch on a small device wired to the panel. Seconds later, the entire facility went dark.

The moment the power went out, the team at the front entrance swung the door open and stepped inside. They spread out and cleared the lobby, then moved deeper inside with short quick steps, keeping their muzzles sweeping for any threats. The well-groomed man monitoring the action saw confusion and panic gripping the employees inside. After a few seconds, the emergency generators kicked in, powering small lights along the walls. Employees laughed nervously and made jokes until they spotted the men with guns.

* * *

The four armed intruders brought their rifles up and fired on everyone they saw. They took disciplined shots with silenced semi-automatic compact rifles loaded with sub-sonic ammunition. Men and women panicked and screamed, trying to flee or warn others, but like a pandemic, the four-man team moved through the area, killing with extreme prejudice. They swept through every corridor, every room, eliminating unsuspecting victims throughout the building.

They reached the server room, and two security guards inside, investigating the blackout, spotted the black-clad soldiers with military gear through the sliding glass entrance. The guards scrambled for cover, drawing their handguns and firing. More panic erupted, as unsuppressed gunfire from the guards' weapons split the air, echoing off of the polished floors and solid walls. Frightened employees inside the room dropped to the floor and scrambled for safety behind the server racks. The team pushed into the server room and spread out. The two men in front switched their weapons to fully automatic, and cut loose with heavy suppressing fire. Big sub-sonic bullets shattered every surface they struck, punching holes through drywall, sheet metal and concrete, keeping the guards pinned.

One of the guards brought his pistol up, firing blind. His weapon bucked wildly as he pulled the trigger until the slide locked back. With shaky hands, he thumbed the magazine release, screaming into the radio on his shoulder. "Repeat, we are under attack. Three or four men with fully automatic weapons have broken in and are—"

His partner's head rocked back from a point-blank shot by one of the intruders. The guard's radio was snatched away by another man. His limbs flailed, and he tried to scoot away, his heart racing. A three round burst punctured his heart and one of his lungs, and his body slumped to the ground, bleeding out.

Two of the black-clad men were shouting and rounding up the employees, herding them to the back of the room. The men and women screamed and cried, begging to be let go. The other pair, a man and woman with strikingly similar facial features, walked to a terminal near the server racks. The woman accessed the servers on the computer while the man set up a portable rig encased in heavy-duty plastic and rubber to protect the small computer from damage during a battle.

The woman typed for a minute, her mouth a tight line of concentration, then she nodded, rotating the monitor of the server terminal to face the man. The display showed a wall of gibberish, nonsense characters and symbols all mashed into one obfuscated mess. He hooked the portable rig into the terminal and entered a few keystrokes. After pressing *Enter*, the display refreshed, showing a directory of files with thumbnail images showing a *snapshot* of the content for each. Another key command brought up a progress bar with the message *Copying files*.

"Retrieving the data now," the hacker with the rig said into his radio.

"Copy that," the reply came a second later. They were all speaking to each other in Russian, now. *"Team three is has completed their objective. Fall back to the rally point once the data is secure."*

"Will do," the hacker replied, as his rig let out a beep, showing the progress bar at 100 percent. He nodded to the other pair, guarding the survivors. With cold efficiency, they began shooting all the hostages, kicking anyone back into the group that tried to flee, before putting a bullet into their skulls. No witnesses. No survivors.

The hacker disconnected the rig, and stuffed the device into his bag, pulling the strap across his body and picking up his weapon. They retrieved several canisters from their own bags, each with a small explosive charge on it. Two canisters were attached to the servers, and another at the entrance of the room. The rest were placed at key points along their path toward the exit.

The Odd Couple in blue-collar uniforms pulled the body of the dead guard from the front gate into the lobby. Everyone was back in the van, and one of the black-clad intruders asked about the fire suppression system.

"Team three disconnected all alarms and disabled the fire suppression systems," The team's leader said. "It's time to move out."

The canisters in the building detonated, the resulting explosions spreading a highly flammable gel everywhere. The flames engulfed the building in a matter of minutes.

The van reached the main gate, slowing long enough to let the imposter guard in, then rolled out casually. Flames and smoke engulfed the entire facility, seeping out through the windows and doors, and began to ignite the exterior.

CHAPTER

2

Two weeks have passed since John Stone saved his goddaughter, Emily, from Warren Ratcliffe. Ratcliffe had Emily kidnapped to force her mother to help him retrieve the *PEST* prototype, a device capable of cracking all forms of digital encryption in real-time. John saved both the mother and daughter, but the device was now in Ratcliffe's possession.

After John rescued Emily in a firefight, which left dozens that tried to stop him dead or injured, he was approached to join a special task force with a mission to retrieve the device and bring to justice those responsible for taking it. Marvin Van Pierce, the Director of the Hostile Response Division, a defense contract company hired by the United States Government, saw great potential in John Stone. Van Pierce's organization and its task force, affectionately referred to by the team members as *The Hard Core*, worked jointly with U.S. Government agencies to counter terrorist activities, both within the borders of the United States, as well as abroad. They were a shadow group, operating with minimal oversight and jurisdictional boundaries of regular government agencies.

Along with John, Director Van Pierce also enlisted the services of Parker Lewis, the computer programmer and self-described hacker that had been caught up in Ratcliffe's plot, against his will. Parker was instrumental in helping John track down the location of the PEST and Stone's goddaughter. Van Pierce's analyst placed Parker's programming and data analysis abilities well above average, but his pattern recognition and spatial reasoning were near-savant levels, making him a valuable member of the new team.

John's ribs ached as he slowly drew in a deep breath, pulling his shoulders back to stretch his muscles. For the past week, after he acclimated to the task force, he worked directly with the team's field agents. They, like him, were men and women with previous military experience. John served in the Army's 75th Ranger Regiment, in the 1st Ranger Battalion, retiring as a 2nd Lieutenant.

The leader of the HRD's task force was Shane Powell, a retired Captain from the U.S. Marine

Corps. He was younger than John, and unlike the retired Army Ranger, Powell transitioned from his military life, right into the *Hard Core*. John and Shane butted heads many times, since the younger man felt his experience was more relevant to today's political climate, and the mission at hand. Still, John respected the Marine and didn't question his decisions in front of the other team members.

Leaning back in the chair and folding his arms across his chest slowly, John eased his joints into position, settling in for the meeting. Parker smiled at John and took the seat next to him.

"So what do you think MVP is going to be talking about today?" Parker asked, using the nickname *MVP* that some of the other members gave to Director Van Pierce.

John kept his eyes toward the front of the room and shook his head slightly. "I don't know." He turned to face Parker. "But I'm hoping he's got more info on Warren Ratcliffe's whereabouts. If his trail goes cold, we're going to have a tough time finding him before he puts the PEST into play."

Marvin Van Pierce walked into the room, followed by Captain Powell and the lead intelligence analyst, Dr. Miranda Spencer. Parker straightened his posture as they took their seats around the table. Dr.

Spencer slid a folder across to John and straightened her coat before settling in her chair.

The Director wasted no time with greetings or other formalities. "Last night, a government-sponsored facility, about seven miles north of Nellis Air Force Base, was destroyed by a fire," he said. "There were no survivors, including the guard at the gate checkpoint, whose body was found inside the building. The fire inspectors have reported there was no doubt that this was arson. On top of that, they have determined everyone inside was already dead before the fire started.

"The fire suppression systems also failed, most likely a result of sabotage. Whoever did this wasn't trying to stage an accident. They were covering their tracks. We don't know what they were after because that facility kept mostly administrative data. Nothing declared top secret or connected to WMDs, but we're working on getting access to what the company was working on."

Dr. Spencer adjusted her glasses. "In the meantime, the fire is the cover story that will be released to the press."

"This might be a stupid question, but what about camera footage. Were the investigators able to recover anything usable?" Parker asked.

Director Van Pierce closed the file folder in front of him. "No footage had been recovered. This facility had state of the art monitoring installed in and around the building, but the connection to remote backup servers had been cut early in the evening. The hard drives with recordings stored locally were destroyed in the fire."

Spencer placed her hands on the table, alternating her gaze between Parker and John. "We currently have no leads. The team that pulled this off is beyond the abilities of anyone we expected to find operating within our borders."

"Outside of sophisticated heist flicks, we have never seen anything like this so expertly executed on a high-security facility," the Director said. "The location and contents of the facility aren't publicly communicated, so we have to assume they've got inside help or a talented team of hackers." He looked over at Parker, narrowing his eyes.

"Ratcliffe," John said. "He's got to be involved."

"There is no evidence connecting Warren Ratcliffe to the team that hit the data storage facility." Dr. Spencer said. "This could be completely unrelated to him and the PEST prototype."

"You're unusually quiet, Mr. Lewis. Cat got your tongue, son?" Van Pierce asked Parker.

"Huh, oh, sorry. Just connecting the dots in my head." He scooped his laptop from the desk and shouldered his backpack. "I've got an idea."

The three other occupants watched as the programmer left the room in a hurry. John and Van Pierce exchanged puzzled glances.

"I'll go with him, sir," Spencer said pushing her chair back in.

"Good idea. Keep him out of trouble," John said as she opened the door.

* * *

"Hey wait," Dr. Spencer said. Her shoes clacked on the polished concrete floor as she struggled to catch up.

"Sorry, Miranda. I just," Parker paused while continuing his hurried pace, "I have an idea how to find out who did this."

"How?" Miranda pushed her glasses up as she reached Parker, matching his pace.

"It's something I did a couple of weeks ago, for John," Parker said. "We tapped into the feeds for cameras all over the city, feeding the data into a program that monitored for patterns that we established."

"Like, real-time? That doesn't help us now."

"Well, this time I was going to pull the recorded data from all systems in the area around that facility. Much easier than trying to spread out a web, like last time." Parker opened the door to the computer lab.

"Is any of that even legal?" Miranda asked.

"It wasn't when John and I pulled it off last time. And since I'm not rotting in prison right now, I'm guessing the brass overlooked it."

"Yeah, you were a fugitive then. You're part of a government-sponsored team now. We can't do that."

"We, or me?" Parker asked, hooking his laptop up to the rest of the network. "Just pretend you didn't say that last sentence, and I'll deal with any heat that drops on my shoulders."

"I can't just," Dr. Spencer searched for the best way to finish her sentence.

"Sure you can. Plausible deniability," Parker said, winking at her as his computer woke.

His fingers snapped in a staccato rhythm, inputting commands, waiting for replies, confirming, and executing. Miranda watched in silence for a few seconds before taking the seat next to his.

"What do you see?"

"Progress," he said, scrolling down a list and selecting various entries as he moved through its contents.

"You've already got something?"

"No, I'm looking at these progress bars down here," Parker said, pointing to the minimized tabs along the lower portion of his computer's display.

Miranda rolled her eyes, sitting back and folding her arms across her chest. "Just let me know when you find anything of interest."

Parker nodded, taking the next few moments to start piping the recorded data into his program, punching in some parameters to narrow his search. He selected the cameras near the facility as the baseline, then moved the perimeter out block by block, each time increasing the number of data points exponentially.

"This might take some time," he said, his voice almost too low to be heard.

"So what, we just wait?" Dr. Spencer asked.

"Yes and no," Parker said, pulling up another browser to start a new search.

Miranda watched him work in silence, one arm still folded across her chest, as she absently chewed on the thumbnail of her other hand.

"The DMV?" she asked when one of Parker's other search results popped up.

"Yeah, I need to cross-reference the vehicles registered to the employees that worked at the facility."

"Whoa, I feel like you're trampling over privacy laws, not to mention my trust." Miranda sat up straight in her chair. "Where are you getting this stuff anyway?"

Parker mumbled as most of the words faded beneath the rapid clicking of his keyboard. The only words she understood were "Freedom of Information Act."

"None of this falls under the FOIA," Miranda said. "You have to submit formal requests to get what you're looking for, not just find a backdoor to the server."

"I made all the necessary requests," Parker said. "I just happened to do it several thousand times per second until I got what we needed."

"We? Don't pull me into this, Mr. Lewis." Spencer stood up.

"Bingo," Parker said, leaning in closer to his screen.

"What? What did you get?" Miranda asked, sitting back down and scooting up closer.

"A few vehicles there that day weren't connected to anyone working at the facility, and only this one was on site close to the time of the fire."

"Is that a maintenance van?" Miranda asked.

"Yeah. I'm not one hundred percent certain, but it looks like the van leaves either shortly before or after the time the fire was called in."

"Can you find out where it went?"

"It's going to take time," Parker said. "The algorithm has to slog through all of the footage as the radius expands. I can try and speed things up by only focusing on the van, but we'll still get plenty of hits for similar vehicles." His fingers flew across the keys again.

Miranda leaned in trying to memorize as much of the vehicle's appearance as she could before getting up from her chair. "I'm going to call in a request for some satellite support."

Parker grunted, continuing to track the van along its possible routes away from the facility, using his program's continuous output. Red lines spiderwebbed out, casting a glowing net at first, but the number of *threads* dropped as the search results expanded. As soon as the program reached twenty-five percent complete, Parker started another program, feeding it the incomplete data from his search.

A new window popped up, building a virtual 3D model of the van he was tracking. On top of the vehicle's color and license plate, the new program used the narrowing tracking results to update the model, adding distinguishing marks, like dents and scratches. With his computer continuing the search in the background and no longer requiring his guidance, Parker focused on the updated virtual model, preparing to send the information to Director Van Pierce and John, letting them know it was the most likely connection to the crew that hit the facility.

Before he could send the email, Parker's program popped up a notification flagging a possible key event. He pulled up the data and reviewed the attached footage. It was from an outdoor convenience store security camera, which caught the van from across the street. The van stopped and a group of men, all dressed in black, got out and moved to an SUV already parked at the location. Unlike the rest of the group, the van's driver and passenger dressed in coveralls. They had a short conversation with one of the men in black fatigues, but they stayed in the vehicle. The SUV and van took off in different directions. Parker cursed under his breath.

"Did you find out where the van went?" Miranda asked, sitting back down, slipping her phone back into a pocket.

"Yes, but we've hit another snag," The tip of Parker's tongue rested on the middle of his upper lip as he rushed to update the search parameters, adding the second vehicle.

"Can I help?" she asked.

"If you can focus on the flagged vid, that would help out," Parker said.

Miranda logged into one of the available computers, accessing the video Parker dropped onto the network. "Uh, what am I looking for? Do you need me to run a facial recognition?"

Parker pulled a thumb drive from his pocket, pinching it between his index and middle fingers. "Use this. Much better than that caveman software everyone is using."

"What is it?" she asked, inserting the drive into an available USB port.

"Mob recognition," Parker said. "It runs through any footage you feed it to identify things like relative height, size, walking gait, stuff like that. All things that facial recognition software doesn't do."

"How is that better than facial recognition?" Miranda asked, selecting the video to drop into Parker's *Mob Recognition* program.

"People have individual traits that set them apart," Parker said. "Not just height and weight, personality quirks that the program catalogs and tracks. It can identify an individual by tracking groups of people."

"How does it do that?"

Parker stopped typing, turning to face Dr. Spencer with a wide self-satisfied grin. "Not only does the catalog keep track of an individual, but also their

Made in United States
Orlando, FL
25 January 2023

29045720R00138